I heard a muffled noise to the right
and turned just in time to catch a
quick glimpse of Proctor in the corner.
He had a gun in his right hand,
and I could make out that Faye
was trapped in his left arm,
his big hand over her
mouth to keep her
from screaming.
He leveled the gun
and fired. . . .

DELANEY
GILBERT MORRIS

LIVING BOOKS
Tyndale House Publishers, Inc.
Wheaton, Illinois

First printing, January 1984
Library of Congress Catalog Card Number 83-51131
ISBN 0-8423-0538-6

1

Most towns are designed by someone who has some concept of traffic flow, but Hot Springs was designed by two lakes—Lake Catherine and Lake Hamilton. They push and nudge at the city, stretching it out like Silly Putty at times, then squeezing it to a ridiculous narrow girth. The shoreline sells for about a thousand bucks a foot and keeps going up.

My heart jumps when I look at one of those lovely million-dollar palaces and realize that ten feet under the surface raw sewage is being pumped into the lake. As a matter of fact Lake Catherine was chosen as one of the ten most polluted bodies of water in the nation. The Arkansas River in Little Rock also made the list. And some folks claim we're backward here in Arkansas! Tush! And also faw!

Once I saw a map of Salt Lake City and have never fully recovered. It's *square!* Half of the streets run south and the other half run east. What an orderly world those Mormons live in! Imagine the thrill of driving straight to your destination!

In Hot Springs, getting from one place to another can be an adventure. I remember one time seeing an armed robbery. I was out cruising, looking for a dinner somewhere that wouldn't chew away my insides. These guys were backing out of a place with money hanging out their pockets. I mean how dumb can you be? If they had just strolled out casually like ordinary shoppers, I'd never have noticed.

They were only a hundred yards away from me. In Salt Lake City I could have driven direct— a nice, fast geometric straight line—and picked them up. But I wasn't in Salt Lake City. I was in Hot Springs, a town that looks like it was designed by a committee. I had to drive in the opposite direction, go down a one-way street the wrong way, and follow a twisting road to the shoreline drive where the holdup was taking place. I should say *had taken* place. I got there five minutes late. The poor shopowner, beaten silly by those crooks, had managed to call the police. I pulled in and he said, "You guys are fast." Yeah.

The traffic plan for Hot Springs is simple; Central runs the length of the city and Grand Avenue crosses it at right angles. If you care to go anywhere on either of those streets, there are possibilities. If you want to go somewhere *not* on one of those streets—leave your forwarding address.

Just to keep things interesting, we have racing season from February through April. Now, to have racing one must have a track, musn't one? And the track must be *somewhere!* And where is Oaklawn? Is it out in the beautiful foothills of the Ouachita Mountains? No. Is it out of the way, somewhere inconvenient for the touts, bookies, and assorted idiots who come from miles away to be fleeced? No.

Oaklawn firmly straddles one of the two main streets that make Hot Springs liveable—Central Avenue. And if one has worked an extra shift out of homicide and is so tired that one's hair hurts, what is there to be done when the length of the avenue is packed with cars filled with hard-working taxpayers waiting for the horsies to cross the street so that the gamblers can watch them run like anything? One sits in the car and watches the needle of the gas gauge sink slowly into the west.

We had worked together in uniform when I first came to the department, but Riley liked the sauce too much and would never be anything more than a third-rate cop. Ah, Riley, how I hate to rise above you!

He finally belched lethally, and grinned like a bilious crocodile: "Well, you probably have to get to your priestly duties, Delaney." He threw up his hand, and some of the trainers looked indignant that their expensive horses had to wait while mere mortals passed.

I got to the shack on the lake that I call home without, as they say in the better eighteenth-century novels, "an interesting incident." The house was actually an oversized storage room for the big, fancy mansion just to the west. Some sort of boundary dispute had resulted in a violent Caesarean operation, separating it from the original parent. I had managed to pay a thousand down and $350.00 a month until the coming of the Apocalypse for the place. It was a wedge-shaped piece of land, like a slice of pie, and the house sat on the tip in the water. It had only one room, a bath, and the smallest kitchen in the Western world. It was enough, though, and I could stand out on the little redwood deck and catch the bass right out of the nicely polluted waters.

I wanted to shower and hit the sack, but such was not to be. I did get the shower, but before I made it to bed the phone rang.

I have two theories about life. Theory Number One is that nothing good in the history of the world ever happened before noon. That's why I sleep until then whenever possible. Theory Number Two is that good news never comes over the phone. I had done all I could to avoid Ma Bell—unlisted phone number, letting it ring ten times, etc. I counted ten rings, then picked it up with intense apathy.

"Yeah?"

"Is that you, Ben?"

"Who else would be answering my phone, Faye?"

"Ben, you gotta come down here right away!"

"No, Faye, I will not come down there."

"But, Ben, there's this guy and he's high on mushrooms—and besides I think he's got a gun or a knife or something, and he may do something crazy, and . . ."

"No, Faye, I will not come down."

I held the phone away from my ear in anticipation of the screech Faye always made when she was crossed. "Call yourself a director! Why you miserable son of—"

There was a scuffle and then Terry's voice: "Ben? I know you must be tired, but it might be better if you could come down."

"What is it, Terry?"

"This black dude is up like you never saw—seeing visions and everything—and, Ben, he is packing heat."

"All right, I'll be there as soon as I can. Now, don't mess with this guy. Let him take the place apart if he wants, right?"

"Sure, Ben, but hurry it a little bit, huh?"

If Terry was spooked it was pretty serious. I hung up and jumped into a pair of faded jeans and covered my Special with a horror of a sport shirt that my Aunt Cleo had given me for Christmas. Usually I dug fishworms in it, but it was dark and I didn't think any of the aldermen would see me. I jumped into the Ford, a 1972 pale green Galaxie with over 250,000 miles on it, and roared out of the driveway. I kept it because it had been converted into the hottest of hot rods by an inept bank robber. He could have made a fortune as a master mechanic, but instead is doing fifteen for robbery in a federal pen. The engine he put in instead of the 351 Cleveland takes up all the room under the hood, and when I nudge the accelerator it makes everyone else want to get out to see why their cars have stopped.

I cut through the back of Oaklawn, scaring the sap out of two purple-haired old ladies going home from the track, then threaded my way through some twisting alleys and back streets until I came out by the fountain. From there it was only two blocks away to the Vine. I parked in front and ran up to the front door, keeping the shirt pulled back from the Special.

Some people have crazies in their families that they're not too eager to talk about, and some have infirmities they'd just as soon ignore, such as a bald head or the heartache of painful psoriasis. I guess the Vine was my own little problem, which is a shame because it does a job that most people would rather sweep under the rug. It's a halfway house for kids on drugs.

I guess every town in the country has one now, and some big cities such as Denver or L.A. have a chain of them. They are nearly always located in an old mansion going to seed in a decaying neighborhood. Usually some of the walls will be knocked out to make a large room for the group meetings, and there will be a raised platform with cheap instruments if it is a religious work.

Most of these places take in young addicts and are operated by ex-dopers, usually pretty young themselves, and a lot of them are ministers of some sort. What I'm saying is that I'm the director of the Vine, and it makes me feel about as out of place as a bullfrog on the freeway with his hopper busted. It's good for a laugh around the precinct, and I get all the nicknames like "Padre" or "Preacher," not to mention "Holy Joe."

Most cops get pretty hard, and only a few that I've known have had any religion beyond the annual Easter visit or an occasional Christmas Eve service. I guess the same could be said of jockeys, truck drivers and roughnecks. Up until a year ago I had no more religion than a groundhog. Then something changed and I found myself saying, "I'm a Christian." It would be no surprise to me if someone stood up, pointed a finger at me, and denounced me for a phony.

I slipped into the foyer just in time to see a huge black guy shove one of the guys into a set of drums, then reach for one of the girls with an arm that looked like a dragline. He grabbed her, jerking her off the floor like Raggedy Ann. It was Faye, and for the first time since she'd floated into the Vine she was speechless.

I moved in close enough to take him from behind, but he must have had radar hearing, because he swiveled his head around, then dropped Faye and pulled a Rapala fillet knife out of his belt. He hollered, "Whitey! I gonna dissect you!"

Snatching the Special out of my belt, I laid it right on his middle, yelling "Hold it right there!" I could have been aiming a potato masher at him for all the effect it had; it didn't scare him any, but I had enough cowardice for both of us.

Some say at times like that their whole life flashes before their eyes. With me it's different. Once in Nam, with a face-to-face shootout with a gook, everything seemed to freeze and sort of roll into slow motion. I seem to have all kinds of time to think and meditate on the situation. Like now, as I looked at that icicle of a blade and the pupils of the mad eyes, inside there was a dialogue going on: "You can't kill him, Ben. He's high and not himself. Maybe down deep he has a lot of good qualities. Maybe he has a silver-haired old mother

11

somewhere in a rocker thinking about her baby boy. With good psychiatric care, a little understanding, and time, why he could be a real fine fellow! Besides, Ben, you're a Christian now, and you know the bit about 'Thou shall not kill.' "

Then things started to roll, and as he thawed out and the blade came a centimeter closer I put all this information into my own personal little computer and got my answer.

I shot him carefully in the thigh.

The heavy bullet jerked the leg back, and I noted with satisfaction that I had missed both the bone and the big artery. He fell on his face and rolled over, grabbing the leg—a 300-pound baby crying for his mama. Getting your leg blown out from under you can take you that way. It did me once. I blubbered like a girl.

Then the noise started, everyone babbling at once. I took off my belt and tightened it around his leg, and he said between sobs, "Thank you! Thank you." We had established a meaningful relationship.

"Terry, call the station and get a car—and have them send the meat wagon over."

Without a word Terry spun his wheelchair around and rolled down the hall to the pay phone.

"He's not going to *die*, is he?" Faye squeaked.

"Yeah, sure he's going to die. We all are."

Then someone said, "You cops! I bet if he hadn't been *black*, you wouldn't have shot him!" I looked over at the side of the room and saw this girl who was glaring at me with loathing.

"No," I said, looking her over. "If he'd been white, I'd have eaten one of his drumsticks."

Policemen get pretty good at putting people in their right little box, but this one wasn't easy. She wasn't a candidate for the Vine—no sign of drugs. But she wasn't quite "right" either. She was a real looker. Tall—about my height which is five ten. Slim, but not *too* slim. She had a Latin color and the flawless skin you almost never see in Anglo-Saxons, and what was even more rare, black hair that hung straight down her back and at least six inches below her belt. Her voice was husky and she had a little wop in her speech.

After the first look I saw that she was on her way down. The playgirls in this town don't keep the bloom long. They get touched, and then like ripe fruit, they begin to go bad fast. The hardness that would cover this girl in about a year was almost invisible now—just a slight coarseness that was just a light in her eye, an edge in the voice, a suggestion in the stance. But she was headed there.

"You're Delaney?" she asked.

"Yes. You want to see me?"

Faye edged in close and said, "This is Gina Romero, Ben. She came in just before that guy came in and busted up the place."

"Isn't there someplace where we can talk?" She looked around the room, and a wrinkle touched her nose as if she smelled bad fish. I could see it was all beneath her—especially me.

Terry wheeled back and said, "They'll be here in a minute, Ben. You going to the station when they book him?"

"They'll take him to the hospital first. Hey— pull him off the rug you guys, before he bleeds all over it." We all grabbed him and put him over the linoleum; he nodded rapidly and kept saying "Thank you! Thank you!"

Terry leaned in closer and got that look in his eyes. "Maybe you ought to go easy on him, Ben. I talked to him a little before he blew up, and he's really had a bad time."

"And if you could keep him here for just a few days, why, maybe something could be done, right?" I laughed and rubbed his head. "You never give up, do you, kid?" I had seen Terry play ball a few times, and he had been something else. He could take a hand off, move easily through a wave of tacklers, then turn on the afterburners and leave only a memory in the arms of the secondary. Now he was nothing but skin, bone, and tendon beneath the waist. I could never look at that, so I always looked into his face. I guess he noticed, but he never said anything.

"Well, we could *try*," he said, grinning.

"Talk about it tomorrow," I said, and started down the hall.

"This way, Gina," I said. She followed me to my office and so did Faye. I stopped outside the door, letting the Romero girl in and blocking Faye as she tried to follow. "I'll give you a full report on the conversation later, Faye," I said smiling. She wheeled and marched off with an angry back, but I knew she'd try to listen in as soon as the door was closed.

I waved the girl to a straight chair, and slumped down behind the battered desk in another one. "What do you want?"

"Well, it's not my idea. Coming here, I mean."

14

She waited for me to apologize but I didn't, so she continued in a less certain tone. "I guess you know my brother-in-law." She paused and then lifted her chin and said loudly, "George Matthews."

I looked out the window into the dusk. There was a squirrel in the pecan tree outside just crazy to rob the birdfeeder. He made his little raid, then marched across the powerline, his cheeks stuffed like suitcases with the loot. "Yeah, I know who he is."

I knew, all right, and so did everyone else in the state. A year earlier there had been a hold-up at a 7-Eleven store. The criminal, for no apparent reason, had blasted a young girl working there. The thing was, she was the sixteen-year-old daughter of Clarence Taylor who owns a large percentage of Hot Springs. He thought even rich kids ought to work, so his daughter took the job before beginning college at Fayetteville. Armed robbery and murder have become kind of common in Arkansas. The murder rate in Little Rock is third highest in the nation; the rape rate is number one. What an achievement.

Taylor had put up a fifty grand reward for the arrest and conviction of the killer. The papers had blown it up. Add to this the movement to bring back the death penalty and a new governor who wanted to prove how tough he was and you'd get the picture. Matthews had been caught and convicted in an almost indecent haste. I'd never even seen him, but any man who can shoot a young girl down for no reason has my permission to die in the chair.

"Well," Gina said with a beautiful sneer, "I guess

you're such a big Christian, you'd like to get him off, right?"

I considered it for about two seconds and smiled sweetly into her face. "I hope they fry the sucker 'til his eyeballs crackle."

Gina jumped a little, and her eyes grew larger. "But I thought that you were all *religious* people here! I knew I could never trust a cop!"

"I know who you do trust, Gina." I had remembered something. She had looked vaguely familiar, and it suddenly came to me where I had seen her. I said, "Larry Proctor." She gave a start at that as if I'd caught her with her hand in the cookie jar.

Proctor was a flashy, jet-set gambler, surrounded by the usual gaggle of bunnies and yes-men. He was a big karate buff and had put a couple of guys in the hospital, including a friend of mine named Maurice Hopper. Maurice ran a little catfish restaurant and we were both woodwork freaks. We got together two or three nights a month to work on furniture, and once we had gone to a three-day craft show in Kentucky. He was a good guy meaning no harm to anyone.

About a year earlier he had a run-in with Proctor in a parking lot over a scraped fender. He wound up in the hospital with his knee on backwards and his ribs busted. Proctor had been hauled down to the station, and I'd noticed the dark girl with long hair, but not much. I'd really been picking out the spot I wanted to hit Proctor in.

She was angry. "You know everything, you cops! Well, let me tell you Larry is better than a lot of you fine religious nuts!"

"Yeah, he's a real prince, Larry is."

She started huffing out, and I didn't care. We were not going to make beautiful music together no matter how much I liked her long hair. She stopped at the door, turned around, and asked in a different voice, "You won't even listen to what I came to say?"

"I'm listening."

She stood there a while, then reluctantly came back and sat down. "Well, I don't have a lot of use for George. He's been a sorry excuse for a husband to my sister. It's hard for me to believe that he killed that girl like they say, but you never know. Anyway, he's going to the chair in eight days. Elizabeth—that's his wife—she's scared to go to the prison, and she's got the kid to keep. He's real sick and she hates to leave him alone. Anyway, I went to see George yesterday; before I left he asked me to come see you. Said he wants to talk to you." She looked at me with that hard light in her eyes. "I guess you won't, will you?"

"Got it right the first time, Gina." I expected her to argue or cuss me out, but she just shrugged her shoulders and got up to leave the room. I got up and followed her out. The squad was there watching the medics load 300 pounds of mushroom addict onto a stretcher, and he was still thanking everyone in sight.

Ray Tennyson was making the arrest. He grinned at me: "No rest for the weary, eh, Preacher? You wanna write it up tonight?"

"Nah. You take care of it, will you, Ray? I'll make the report tomorrow."

Just then a kid came in the front door, looked

around, and went over to take Gina Romero by the hand. "Aunt Gina, I'm tired of waiting in the car. He looked up into her face and pulled at her to go. He was a thin kid wearing the usual— sneakers, T-shirt with the Mighty Hulk sneering at the world, faded jeans. I could see a resemblance between the two, but there was something frail about the boy. He had bright brown eyes, but there was that intangible look that chronically sick people have.

"Come on, Elvis," Gina said, and pulled him to the door. Something prompted me to follow them outside; I caught up to them on the sidewalk. Gina stopped and said coldly, "Well, what is it?"

"Is this the boy?"

"Yes. Elvis, this is Mr. Delaney."

He looked at me in the way kids have when they're sizing up an adult, and I felt that I was being weighed in the balances and found wanting, but then he smiled and his face lit up like a sign. "Hi," he said and stuck out his hand.

"Hi, yourself," I said. His hand was like a fragile bird. Tiny bones. "Mind if I talk to your Aunt Gina for just a second?"

"Sure," he said, then with a quick motion he scurried toward the parked car, got in, and turned the radio up full blast.

Gina was watching me curiously. "What's this all about?"

"How old is the boy?"

"He'll be six day after tomorrow."

"His illness—is it serious?"

She pursed her full lips in a way that could be distracting. "Leukemia. The doctor says he won't make it." For the first time that night the hard sheen left Gina's eyes, and there was a softness in her lips as she looked toward the car, then back at me. "I got the idea that he had given up on the kid." She turned her head to one side and inspected me closely. "What difference?"

I couldn't tell her that Elvis was the same age as my own boy would have been if he had lived. And I couldn't tell her it was my fault he was dead. And I couldn't tell her that Elvis had that same piping voice, and the same easy way with adults that I had begun to see in Scott before he died.

"I'll go see your brother-in-law." Fat lot of good it would do, I thought. The guy is already dead except for the actual execution.

I had confused her. "Well-thanks."

"Where can I get in touch with you?"

"I'm a—" she caught herself, then ended the sentence, "I work at the White Orchid." It was one of the clubs in town that operated on the thin edge of legality. She fished a piece of paper out of her purse and scribbled a number on it. "You can call me at this number at home."

She gave it to me and smiled. I saw that there was a very nice person beneath that playgirl exterior. Too bad. She wouldn't be there long—not with Larry Proctor writing her script.

2

Lake Catherine and the Arkansas River aren't the only polluted spots in Arkansas; there's Tucker and Cummins, the two prison farms. Every five years or so we have a red-hot scandal over the inhuman treatment of prisoners, and usually a warden is fired or a governor rides in on the reform ticket. Nothing much ever changes in the system, though, and there's always a new horror awaiting the next exposé. There's the "Tucker Telephone"—a set of alligator clips wired to electricity and clamped on the most tender parts of the body. The last time around there was a 300-pound guard with a twenty-foot blacksnake whip and a face like a Nazi commandant. This year was a little different. A secret cemetery was discovered close to Cummins and you just won't believe how puzzled and shocked the former guards and administrators were about the whole thing. One of them kept insisting it was an old Indian burial ground, but the credibility gap widened when one of the battered bodies emerged wearing a Timex on its remaining arm.

It was late afternoon when I drove up to Cummins, just a few miles out of Pine Bluff. It's profoundly unimpressive—just a group of single-story concrete buildings surrounded by a high hurricane fence surrounded by a thousand acres of flat cotton land. The guard who manned the guard tower treated me politely enough, but when I got inside and made my way to the shakedown room, the hard-eyed guard who asked me to divest myself of all metal objects before passing through the electric eye, gave a poor imitation of Humphrey Bogart. I always liked Bogie, though, so I remained relatively unafraid of his stare and tight-lipped instructions. Finally he assured himself that I wasn't smuggling a trench mortar in to the Count of Monte Cristo, and said, "Down that hall—to your right." I passed a few inmates in the hall; something about their white uniforms bothered me. I suppose I expected the black-and-white stripes from old George Raft movies. I supposed most of them worked on the prison farm, because their faces were burned very dark by the sun, but beneath that was an inner darkness that was somehow frightening.

I found the door marked *Warden*, and after a hulking white-garbed trusty checked my identification, he spoke into the intercom in a fine tenor voice: "Warden, can you see Officer Delaney from Hot Springs? He has an appointment."

"Send him in!" The voice seemed to come through the heavy oak door rather than over the speaker, and when I passed through into the inner office I saw that the man fit the voice. Warden Findley was built along the lines of a Russian Olympic power lifter, massive as an oak tree and with a face that shouted "No!" in every line.

"I'm Ben Delaney." I gave him my best smile and a Dale Carnegie handshake. The smile bounced off harmlessly, and he returned my hand after mashing it in a Stilson wrench grip. I was hopeful that the feeling would return in time. "Warden, I called you earlier about seeing George Matthews."

Warden Findley was not charmed. He sat down and began to look through a file on his desk, then he glanced over the top of it with eyes like pistols. I was glad that I wasn't a prisoner asking for special favors. "Whithersoever the carcass is, there the buzzards will gather together," he said. "Every time we have an execution up here the 'visitors' start dropping by: writers, do-gooders, just plain curiosity seekers. What's with you, Delaney?"

I shrugged and lied easily; this was no time to tell the truth—and Warden Findley was not the man to tell it to. I had the feeling that doing Findley out of an execution would be a little like depriving a tiger of a sirloin. "Well, Warden, you know how it is with cops. There's a case that I've been working on for a year or so, and I think Matthews might have something for me. Might be a promotion in it for me, you know?"

It was the kind of selfish thinking that Findley could understand—after all he might get another execution out of it. "All right, you can see him. But he's not on the Row."

I was surprised. Condemned felons are kept in a special set of cells called the Row for the last week. "Why not?" I asked.

"He's been sick for the last day or two. We've got him in a special room in the infirmary."

"Sounds like it might be a good way to bust out."

I think there was a gleam of humor in the Warden's obsidian eyes. "Nope. He's more secure there than in the Row. I thought he was faking at first, but we've got a pretty good doc here who says it's for real." He showed his teeth in a strange smile. Very shark-like. "When you get there you'll see why I'm not worried about an escape." He rang a bell and a trusty in white stepped inside almost before it stopped ringing.

"Nelson, take this man to see Matthews. Wait 'til he's finished, then show him out."

"Yes, sir, Warden." He was a skinny little guy with a bad tic in his right eye, and he disappeared so quick I almost missed seeing him go.

"Thanks a lot, Warden," I said and stuck out my hand which he studied then went back to his folders. I took the hand out with me when I left and followed Nelson down the long corridor through a series of steel doors that were opened by guards. Nelson walked so fast I had to stretch my legs to keep up with him. "What's the rush, Nelson?" I gasped. "You late or something?"

"Warden Findley don't like for us to mess around," he whispered. Then he shot a furtive look around and said, "You got a smoke?"

"No, I don't use 'em—but have some on me." I handed him a buck which disappeared magically into his loose white garment. "Does it bother you guys much when there's an execution?"

"Naw—only them on the Row." He stepped up the pace to a slow trot and whispered, "Can you take a letter out for me—I got it right here."

"Now, Nelson, what would Warden Findley say about that?" I was only kidding a little and had half a notion to take the letter out, but Nelson suddenly whirled and grabbed at me. His face was tight and his eyes were bright with fear and desperation.

"Don't tell the Warden, Mister—please! I—I only got sixteen more months and I kept my nose clean all the time!" His voice broke and what little manhood was left began to leak out as he sobbed and grasped at my clothing. I was ashamed, somehow, for him, for me, and for the kind of system that emasculated a man so utterly.

What a nightmare of a world—these prisons! They shove a first offender, fifteen years old, into a cell with three hardened criminals. He gets raped. In the yard or in the block, there's a tiger in every dark corner waiting to rip him to bits if he refuses to sink to the level of feral animalism. There in the dark shadows he must grope his way through every perversion that crazed, twisted minds can invent in the long useless hours in the block. And if he complains to the guards, they only laugh, most of them, and throw him back to the wolfish inmates who are likely to make his life even more hellish for his attempts to keep himself human.

In one of Cousteau's movies, there was a school of sharks following a fishing vessel for the offal.

One of the sharks was injured and as his entrails began to trail along, his grinning brothers began to snap at them, devouring him alive. And what was even worse, the injured shark himself began to turn and snap at his own intestines, devouring himself. I always thought of that scene every time I visited a prison.

I caught at Nelson's arms, thin as broomsticks, holding him still for a minute. Then I said gently, "Hey, man, I'm *sorry!* I was just kidding, and that was stupid of me. Just give me the letter and I'll see it gets mailed."

He jerked his arms away and rolled his thick lip back from his yellow teeth. "Letter? I don't know nothing about no letter." If looks could kill I would have dropped dead right there, but there was no way to talk to him. He nearly ran to the next checkpoint, and when I passed through the steel gate he was giving a note to the guard. "Warden says to let this guy see Matthews."

"OK, Nelson. Sit over there." The guard was as fat as Nelson was skinny, and an old image of Laurel and Hardy skipped across my mind. "You can come this way—after I check you out." He ran his hands down my sides and checked me over for hardware, but I had left the Special in the glove compartment. "You can talk to the prisoner but you can't touch him or get close enough to pass him anything. Come on." He led me through steel doors that dropped into place behind us. I could see through the small glass windows six or seven beds in rooms, and most of them were unoccupied. Finally we got to the end, and there was another guard tilted back in a cane chair with a sawed-off Browning across his lap which he allowed to drift in my direction.

"Visitor to see the prisoner," Fatso said, and the armed guard nodded slowly, pulling a thick key from his pocket. He unlocked the door and nodded toward the bed across the room.

"You set thar," he said in a typical delta drawl, "and if you get close to the prisoner, I'll blast yore guts out."

I looked at him, and he obviously meant every word. "Nicely put, old man."

There was a commode, a lavatory, and a bed. Nothing else. The man on the bed was about five-eleven and if he had been in good condition, would have weighed about 175. Sickness had stripped the flesh away, leaving little folds and a dewlap under his bony chin, and there was a dullness of eye that I had seen in Nam so often in the faces of those that had decided to die. He didn't seem surprised to see me although I didn't think they had told him I was coming.

"I'm Ben Delaney," I said and sat down in the cane-bottomed chair. I saw that the shotgun guard was looking at us through the thick glass window. "Your sister-in-law says you want to see me."

Matthews nodded slowly and hunched his shoulders together as if he were cold and trying to get warm. "Yeah, I told her that," he said. He looked at me but I could see that he was dulled somehow, as if he were on a downer. When he finally spoke again, I noticed that his voice was raspy like he had bronchitis. "Thanks for coming."

"What was it you wanted to see me about, Matthews?"

"Well, I guess you know that in eight more days they're going to kill me."

"Well—yes," I answered. How could that stark fact be put in any more acceptable form?

He seemed to be ill at ease, and I couldn't think what sort of situation could made a dead man uncomfortable. Finally he looked at me and his eyes lit up with a fire that glowed through the dullness. "Delaney, I got to tell you something."

"Go right at it, George," I said.

"I didn't do it."

Well, there it was—what I had hoped not to hear. I sighed and said, "I know, you were framed, weren't you?"

"You don't believe me."

"You know, George, I've been a cop for about ten years, more or less—and I've just never met any real criminals. They're all innocent victims of society. Or else they were temporarily insane."

George came alive then and shook his finger in my face. "I don't care *what* you've seen, cop! I *know* I didn't hold up that place, and I didn't kill nobody!" Then he suddenly stopped and a film seemed to drop over his eyes, putting out the fire. He hunched his shoulders together and shivered a little as he added, "I didn't think anyone would believe me."

Then it happened. For absolutely no reason I *did* believe him! Me! I'd heard experts explaining their innocence, orators who could twist the heart with their voices and who could sway the emotions with their drama—and I hadn't been fooled often. But somehow the very hopelessness of Matthews caught at me.

"But you *confessed*, George!" I said loudly to still that crazy impulse to believe him. "You went over the whole thing in open court. You *couldn't* have known all those details if you hadn't done the job."

"I didn't do it, Delaney," he mumbled.

"Then *why* did you confess—and how did you know every detail?" I had gone over the transcripts and never in my life did I know of a man so anxious to get himself convicted as George Matthews. Why, he ran *ahead* of the prosecutor with his confession! It was as if he were afraid he *wouldn't* be convicted. Yet even now looking into his dumb face I still had the eerie, unreasonable feeling that he was innocent.

"Delaney," he said, and there was more life in his voice, "I know it looks bad, and I don't reckon there's anything to be done now—but I wanted someone to know I didn't do it." He leaned toward me and whispered, "Will you let me tell you how it was?"

"I'm here," I sighed. Half of my mind was saying, *Don't be a sucker, Ben!*—but there was still something that said, *He didn't do it.*

"It was like this, and I ain't told this to nobody—not even Elizabeth. About a year ago I started getting real sick. I went to the doctor and took all kinds of medicine, but I just got worse. Then one day I went in and they done a bunch of tests and after that the Doc told me I had something bad wrong—I forget the name of it—and that there wasn't no cure for it."

"Why didn't you tell Elizabeth?"

"What for? I thought maybe the Doc was wrong, but anyways we got this kid, and he's been real sick for a long time, and no insurance or nothing."

"Wait a minute," I interrupted. "All this happened a year ago. There must have been some way to get help. There are organizations that help people in trouble."

He looked down at his hands and mumbled, "Yeah—well don't ask me, Delaney. Seems like there wasn't no line of folks tryin' to help me out."

"Didn't you have any family to help you out?"

"Naw, we ain't a very close family."

"Well, what did you do then, George?"

"I had nearly $500 saved up that Elizabeth didn't know about. So the only thing I could think of was maybe get in a big game and make a bundle so Elizabeth and the kid would have some money after I kicked the bucket. So what I done was take the dough and hang around the Arlington Hotel and get in one of the poker games with the big shots."

"You couldn't get in one of those, George. They're pretty careful about who they play with."

"Sure, but I got a friend who helps set them up, and I slipped him fifty and he got me in all right, but—" he paused then looked at me with a harried look on his lean face. "I didn't last long. About five hands and they cleaned me out."

"Not surprised. What then?"

He scrunched down in the cot and looked up at the ceiling before he answered. "Well, I seen that one of them was the big winner, so I just sort of went outside to the parking lot and waited around 'til he come out. Then finally he did and he was all alone. I figgered I couldn't lose noways, so I put a gun on him and got his roll."

"But you didn't keep it, did you, George?"

"No—and I never figgered it out. One minute I had the gun on him and the money in my hand, and the next minute I'm on the cement and he's got all the marbles. I don't think I even seen him move!"

I shook my head in pity. "These big time gamblers are pretty hard, George. They have to be. You're lucky he didn't split your wishbone."

"Am I?" he grinned suddenly. "I wouldn't be here, would I? But you know, he didn't seem too surprised to see me. I think he had it all figgered out that I'd be there."

"Wouldn't have been too hard for a sharp operator to see."

"Yeah—but you know what, he wasn't mad at me or nothing. Why, he put the gun in his pocket and then we got to talking and the first thing you know we wuz in a bar and I was telling him all about my problem. You know it was sorta like I was confessing like to a priest." He shook his head at the memory. "He sure did suck me in."

"What did he look like, George?"

"Oh, he was a big guy, you know? About fifty, maybe fifty-five and a sharp dresser!"

"Had you ever seen him before?"

"Nah! I'd have remembered him! He said his name was Ralph Felton." He thought a minute and said, "I'd know him if I saw him again, though!"

"What did you talk about?"

"A lot of stuff, but you know, when I told him about me being a dying man why it sort of got to him like. I mean he got real interested and I could see he was—touched by it, I reckon. And then that's when he come up with the deal."

"What deal?"

"The whole deal to get the reward—the reward for the guy that killed that girl,—you know about that."

Light was beginning to break through. "Wait, let me tell you, George. You would confess to the murder and get yourself convicted; this guy would collect the reward and split it with you. Then after you were dead, Elizabeth and the kids would have money to live on, right?"

George's mouth flew open and he stared at me as if I had just eaten my own head, and he said breathlessly, "You're a smart one, ain't you!"

"And now you're here and the reward has been paid—and you never saw any of it, did you, George?"

He dropped his head and didn't say anything for a long time; then he lifted his eyes to me and they were dim with tears. "I ain't smart, Delaney. Never have had any sense. Never been worth a damn to anybody. I just thought that once in my life I might do some good for Elizabeth and Elvis. But I was too dumb, wasn't I?"

Somewhere there was a guy spending fifty big ones. He was driving a Lincoln, eating at Cajun's Wharf with the bunnies that swarm to the loot. He slept good nights, and if he ever thought of the poor slob that he had maneuvered into the Row at Cummins, he probably got a kick out of it. I could almost see his face—sleek, well-fed, glowing with success and health.

And I was going to nail him to the wall.

Or so the impulse took me. I have these little fantasies sometimes. Often I am John Wayne leading the troop to the last survivors of the wagon train before the savage Apaches make pincushions out of them. Then again I am Batman with the trusty Robin at my side, righting the wrongs of villainous criminals. This Walter Mitty aspect of Delaney is usually kept carefully hidden from the public, for I have several puckered scars—results of terminal idealism. Still, the face of Matthews—dumb, hopeless, and thin—triggered that familiar anger that usually got me shot or mashed with blunt instruments.

"There ain't no use is there, Delaney?" George asked.

I took a deep breath and plunged in—Captain Marvel against the forces of evil! "I'm going to try, George. It's probably too late, but if you'll give me all you know, I'll take a shot at it." His eyes lit up, and I held up my hand. "George, you can't count on this. Maybe there's one chance in a million—not more. I think you'd better—I mean, you might as well,—" then I sort of trailed off into a meaningless series of mumbles. I guess I thought I should tell him to get ready to meet God, but I was embarrassed at saying things like that to other people.

He grinned and said, "Yeah, I know. I read in the paper about you getting on the glory road and all that. Look, don't worry about me. I—I'm just glad you believe me."

I got out my note pad to cover up my sudden confusion. "OK George, give me what you got—*all* of it."

He went through it all—several times—but the only thing that sounded hopeful was the confession. "When I asked him how I could be sure I would get my part of the money, he said that he'd sign a confession and that I could blackmail him with it if he didn't pay up. So he wrote it all down and put it in an envelope and we went to the bank the next day and I put it in a safe deposit box."

I asked what was to me a logical question. "How did you know he gave you his real name?"

He looked at me helplessly. "I never even thought of it."

I got up and put the pad away. "George, I'll do my best. And I'll probably see your family tomorrow. Anything you want me to tell them?"

"I guess not. There ain't much sense in talking about the weather at this stage, is there?" He rolled over and put his face to the wall and I left him there.

As I mulled it over driving back home one thing was clear: whoever *collected* the reward wouldn't be that gambler. He was too sharp for that!

First, you find out who got the money. Then you get him in some dark alley and beat out of him who he gave it to. Then you find *him* and make him confess to the whole thing in open court. What could be simpler than that?

But it wouldn't be like that. It never was. There are two kinds of crooks—dumb ones and smart ones. And the dumb ones are so easy it's almost a shame to take them—but the smart ones are almost never caught because they're survivalists at all costs. And this one was *real* smart. He could think fast, and he could innovate. He had time on his side, because if I didn't nail him in a week he was off the hook for good.

The only thing I had going was a rousing hatred for Mr. X. It was like a burning in my belly. I got it for drug pushers, wife-beaters, child molesters, embezzlers of helpless elderly people, and dog poisoners. Most of the time it left my mind clear and functional, but there were times when it fell across my eyes like a red curtain and let something deep in me take over.

I almost got that way now thinking of Elvis's face. Mr. X had somehow struck at the boy, and even though my reason told me that he couldn't have known of the boy, something deep in me cried out like a savage with war-paint streaked across his face: "Get him!"

And as the car split the darkness, I agreed with my baser nature that the proper thing to do was to turn over rocks until I found this persecutor of orphans and strip him so bare that the buzzards would have to go hungry.

In a nice Christian way, of course.

3

Prisons and city jails seem to exude some sort of aroma that clings to me. Maybe it's the fear seeping through from the trapped animals in some kind of osmosis. Anyway, I can never get it off even with a scalding shower; it always takes a few days for the smell to fade away.

By the time I got home and took a long shower, I had decided to follow up on Matthews's story. I dialed the number that Gina Romero had given me and a young voice answered cautiously.

"Hullo?"

"Hello. Is Gina Romero there?"

"Hullo?"

"Is this Elvis?"

"Yes."

"Elvis, would you get your Aunt Gina for me, please?"

He didn't answer but there was the sound of departing steps, and in a few moments Gina's voice answered, "This is Gina."

"Delaney."

"Oh, well—" She seemed surprised to hear from me.

"I have to talk to you, Gina."

"Right now?"

"Yeah, right now."

"But I've got a date—"

"You've got a brother-in-law who's going to fry in a week." I snapped. "What's your address?"

"Well, it's 2410 Baker, but—"

"I'll pick you up in fifteen minutes." She sputtered, but I cut her off and left the house.

The idiots were still at Oaklawn watching the horsies run around in circles, so getting across town was easy. I turned off on Grand Avenue and drove to Baker Street. The house was on the corner—a one-story frame that would have been white if anyone had bothered to paint it. Like the rest of the houses in the neighborhood, it was tired, leaning against time rather wearily. "Grand Avenue ain't so grand," I muttered as I parked between an ancient Datsun and a late model Camaro. The Camaro seemed out of place; it was light blue with all the trimmings, and still in its first year. A woman's car, which I deduced from the package of Kleenex on the dash—you know my methods, Watson—and I guessed it would belong to Gina.

There was no doorbell, and when I knocked on the peeling paint it was opened at once by a heavy middle-aged woman with hair that just *couldn't* decide which color it wanted to be.

"Yes? What is it?" she asked in a low voice. I couldn't see too well through the screen, but the glimpse I got showed me that she had the same general features of Gina Romero—far gone in fat and worry. If she lost thirty pounds and took a restful vacation and made about ten major adjustments she would have the good looks of her sister.

"I'm Ben Delaney. Gina is expecting me."

"Oh, sure," she muttered. She opened the door, shooing the flies away wearily. "I'm Elizabeth Matthews. Come on in." I followed her into the room and found myself in the main living area. No wasting any space on anything useless like a foyer or entrance for them. The inside was as grim as the outside. Cheap paneling and discolored tile on the ceiling. A lot of sad furniture that had once graced the floor of Sears or Penneys and had been defeated by time and chance. She waved to a chair and said, "Gina won't be long. Have a seat."

"Thanks." I avoided the steel spring that poked up like a bayonet out of the overstuffed chair, and looked at Elizabeth Matthews.

"Are you gonna help George?" she asked suddenly, and I saw that helpless look that relatives have when they ask the doctor, "Is he gonna be all right, Doc?" when they know deep down that he *isn't* gonna be all right.

I shifted nervously and thought bad thoughts about Gina, who had probably said too much to Elizabeth. "Well, Mrs. Matthews, I'm going to look into a few angles about your husband's case—but I wouldn't want you to expect much. It's pretty—late." I ended falteringly.

Elizabeth nodded heavily without any hope in her faded eyes. "I know—it ain't no use. Seems

39

like it's happening to somebody else. Oh, George ain't been no *prize*, but it just don't seem possible that he *killed* that girl." She turned to leave and said, "Well, I gotta get back to the kitchen. Gina won't be long." She looked at me again and smiled briefly. "Anyways, thanks for trying." She plodded off and I was depressed as I always am in the presence of the wives of criminals.

I think the families of criminals have it just as bad as the men who are locked up in the cells. Nothing much to hope for except the release, and most of them will be back only for a short time. It's almost like the prison is their home, and they get out once in a while just to visit their families, then they have to commit another crime so they can get back to their *real* home. And with Elizabeth Matthews there wasn't even this phantom to hope for.

"Can you play checkers?" I jumped a little for I hadn't heard a sound. Elvis had floated in and was standing right at my side with a checkerboard in his thin hand. He was so close I could see the fine blue veins in his wrist and I noticed again that he seemed almost insubstantial. But his face was clear—bright eyes and a hopeful expression on his lips.

"Can I play checkers?" I asked in mock surprise. "Kid, you're talking to the three-time champion checker player of Lakeside High School." I pulled a shaky end table in front of me and took the board from him and put it down. "Do you want red or black?"

"I like the red ones," he said and pulled a livid orange hassock up close. "But you can have the red if you want."

I watched him line the men up quickly, and answered, "No, I like the black ones. You get first move."

"OK," he said and his face got very serious. He immediately moved a checker and looked up at me expectantly. He had dark eyes, but they seemed to have some sort of light flakes of color in them. I moved and he immediately moved another piece.

"You're not fooling around, are you, Elvis? Now you better be careful, because, like I say, I'm no man to mess with on the checkerboard."

He was very serious and as we played I was fascinated to see his eyes light up when he jumped a man or when he was trying to maneuver me into a trap. He was good, all right, and at one point I thought I had him trapped. But he suddenly looked at me with a quick smile and snapped up three of my pieces, beating me before I knew what was up.

"Say, you've played this game before," I protested.

He grinned at me. "I can beat my daddy sometimes." He sobered for an instant and asked, "Do you know my daddy?"

"Well, not really, Elvis. But I think I'm going to see him pretty soon."

"He's in jail." The thin boy took his eyes off me and slowly pushed a checker around the board, then looked back with his eyes glistening. "Can I go with you when you go see him?"

"Well, I don't think it would be—" I bogged down and was glad to hear footsteps coming down the short hall. Gina entered and I said quickly,

"Well, we have to go, Pal. Maybe I'll practice up and we can play another game of checkers—OK?"

He nodded and said, "I'd like that. What's your name?"

"This is Mr. Delaney, Elvis," Gina said. "He is going to—"

"Well, we'll see you soon," I said hurriedly, and dragged Gina out of the room.

"What's the hurry!" she protested.

"I didn't want you telling the boy any stories with endings like 'They lived happily ever after,' " I said, releasing my hold. "Get in."

"Where are we going?"

"I'm hungry. Any place special you want to eat?"

"I guess not."

She clammed up and I knew she was sore at the way I had pressured her. I drove past all the fast food places with the shudder I always have when I see their neon promises. The pizzas, hamburgers, chickens, tacos, and a dozen others all soaked in grease and pulverized past recognition. Sometimes I watched the yokels introducing those abominations into the delicate linings of their stomachs and felt that the doom of America was nowhere more obvious than this deviation from wholesome cooking.

The Catfish House was almost invisible, hidden behind a large Safeway store not far from the fountain. There was no neon, just a small sign that said FRESH CATFISH DINNERS with a single 60-watt bulb over it. I parked on the street and led Gina inside. It was almost full as usual, and I knew most of the customers. A few of them looked up from their plates and said, "Hello, Delaney" as we walked toward the rear. Maurice met me and stuck out his hand. He was a short, dark guy with warm brown eyes and a feeling for people that kept him pretty well skinned up economically, socially, and physically. He was one of the few people that I trusted without reservation.

"Hey, Ben, you ain't been in for a week!" he said, pumping my hand furiously.

"Had to get over the last ptomaine your fish gave me." I ducked the short punch that he always threw at me. "This is Gina Romero, Maurice."

"Hey, glad to see you," he smiled. "Come on, your table was just set up." He led us to the rear of the small building to a little nook that had a table big enough for four and we sat down. "Be right back with you guys," he said and zipped off. A waitress appeared and set the salad and hush puppies on the table.

"No menu?" Gina asked.

"Don't need one," I said between bites of the crispy hush puppies. "This is Maurice's Catfish House. You come here to eat catfish. You want anything else you go somewhere else." I couldn't resist the food. The hush puppies were made with beer and seasoned just right as always, and I had to keep from filling up on them until the fish came. The waitress put a small platter with six pieces of fish on it, and I tore into one. "Try a bite," I waved at the platter.

Gina hesitated, but I knew how the smell of that fish could ruin your character and good intentions. "Is this all the fish you get?" She picked up a piece and bit into it. I enjoyed the way her eyes

43

opened wide. "Say! This is *good!*" she said in surprise. Like most of her type she thought all food had to be served in a million-dollar joint with lots of lights and schmaltzy music.

"They only bring out six pieces at a time," I explained. "Stays hot that way. You know, that fish was alive an hour ago."

"It was!"

"Yeah. Maurice keeps the fish alive in a stainless steel tank—right out through that door. Most of the fish places serve you a fish that was grown on fertilizer and was killed and packed a week before you ever see it on a platter. Here, try one of these hush puppies."

"Well, I have to eat later on—but just *one* wouldn't hurt, I guess. They are so *good!*" I grinned to myself and sure enough she couldn't quit, and before long we were measuring bite for bite, and I think she put me in the shade. I never saw a girl eat so much. Finally we sat back and breathed a little. I watched her as she drank some of Maurice's good brewed coffee, and when she was full and relaxed I began to lay it out for her.

"Gina, I'm not gonna kid you, it's a million-to-one shot that we could help George."

Her eyes snapped at me. "I *knew* it! You're gonna weasel out of it, ain't you?"

I shook my head sadly. "You've been watching too much TV. You think that those cops you see on the tube are real. Now, I'm gonna tell you, Gina, Kojak wouldn't last two days on the worst police department in America." She started to protest but I overrode her. "It's not a fairyland, and crimes don't get solved by a magic wand or by a detective who ignores all the rules. Perry Mason won over three hundred cases right there in the courtroom—but if you were ever in a criminal court you'd laugh your head off at ole Perry! It just isn't that way, Gina. I wish it were."

"Aren't you gonna do *anything*?" she asked and bit her lip nervously.

"Yeah, I'm gonna do *something*—but I'm telling you now it's probably too late. I don't want you telling the boy that the Great Detective is going to get his dad out of Death Row."

"I didn't—" she began, then reddened a little. "Well, the poor little guy hasn't got much going for him, sick and all that. I just thought it might give him a little hope."

"Maurice, gimme the phone, will you?" I took the extension and plugged it into the jack. "Sure, I know, but how would it be if you got his hopes up and then everything went *clunk*?" I dialed the station, and Peterson answered.

"Farley? Delaney. Listen, is Manning there?"

"No, but Sonny is just leaving. You want him?"

"Yes, get him to the phone, will you, Farley?" I waited until I heard my partner's voice and said, "Sonny, I got a quick one for you. Run down one Ralph Felton. Supposed to be a high-roller. Tall, heavy-set, maybe 200 pounds, silver hair, dark skin. Was in a big game at the Arlington Hotel about six months ago. See if he's got a record, hey?"

"Delaney, I was on my way to the lake—but I'll get it for you. You want to call in?"

"No, I'll be at the Vine for the next hour, or maybe at the cabin."

"O.K. I'll check it."

I got up heavily and said, "Come on, let's get out of here." I tipped the waitress too much and fended off Maurice with a promise to meet him early in the week for some golf. We were almost to the car, when Gina said, "He seems like a nice guy."

"Maurice?" I looked at her as she settled down in the seat of the car. "Yeah. Did you notice he limps a little?"

"Yes. Was he crippled or did he have an accident?"

"I guess you would say it was an accident. He tried to stop a guy from pushing a parking attendant around and he got beat up by Larry Proctor. He wasn't satisfied by knocking Maury down—he had to kick his kneecap until it got all smashed."

"That wasn't Larry who did that," she protested quickly. "He's a tough guy, but he wouldn't do that."

I shrugged, drove down Central and started to drive her home. If she needed Proctor, I wasn't going to convince her what a klutz he really was.

"I don't have to be at the club for nearly an hour. Can't I go with you? I mean, didn't you tell the guy to call you when he finds out about Felton?"

I was in a box, because I didn't want her along. "I've got to go down to the Vine, and I don't think you'd enjoy it. It's just a—a sort of service that the kids have every night. A religious service."

"I want to know about Felton," she insisted. "You won't be long, will you?"

"No, but I don't really think we'll find out anything tonight."

She settled back into the cushion and said, "It won't kill me I guess. You can take me to the club later."

We got to the Vine and I was still uncomfortable. We went inside and the kids were milling around in the big room getting ready. Terry wheeled up and said, "My, you're on time for once. Hi, Gina. Good to see you." He circled around and called the crowd together. "OK you guys, hold it down, will you?" The crowd settled down, about fifteen of them, and Terry picked up his guitar and said, "Let's just sing for awhile, OK?"

He could have made it in show business, Terry could. His fingers slid up and down the frets, easy, but firm, and unlike the amateurs, the notes were never single, isolated. They met and melted into each other, then separated and faded out into another sound. Like all of the good ones, Terry sounded like two or even three guitarists playing together, but nothing showy like Glen Campbell or Feliciano with their flashy runs. Just smooth and easy. Pretty soon there was that little surge of feeling when the kids joined Terry's smooth baritone, and even I made a try. Terry moved from one chorus to another, and I glanced over at Gina out of the corner of my eye. She was a little tense, but I saw she was impressed at the good sound. I guess she expected the old time Salvation Army band with the off-key trombone and bass drum.

The singing didn't last long. Terry laid his guitar down and pulled a black Bible out that looked like it had come over on the Mayflower. Every page was scotch-taped and the cover was a joke. I could never get over the way he would just mention a verse and that old black Bible would just seem to sort of *flop* open right at it every time. As for me, I was still having trouble finding the maps.

"Just one word tonight, you guys," he said. "You've heard it before and you'll hear it again. In the third chapter of John" (the old Bible did its stuff and flopped open right to the place), "this guy came to Jesus and started to talk with him. Now he was real religious, this Nicodemus, and he started beating around the bush, but Jesus really laid it on him. He said, 'Look, Nick, you gotta start out all over again. You ain't making it, you know? I mean, like you gotta be *born again.*'"

The way Terry went at it was something! It just sort of came to life right there in the Vine. The old Jew with degrees from all the seminaries and the young Jew from Nazareth sitting there in the dark. And the story went on and you could see from the way Terry laid it out that this Nicodemus for all his religion had missed it somehow. I'd heard it all, and so had most of the young addicts, but Gina hadn't. She was almost hypnotized, leaning forward, forgetting all about who she was.

Pretty soon Terry had finished, and he just said quietly with a warm light in his eyes, "So Nick bumped into the Carpenter from Nazareth, and he found out that the God he thought he knew just wasn't there."

"Say, Terry, what ever happened to that Nicodemus?" one of the group asked.

"Hard to say," Terry answered. "He's only mentioned one more time in the Bible, and you can't really say if he went on with Jesus or not." He let the silence run on, then said, "Well, let's just close with a prayer, all right?" And then he prayed a very short prayer while we all stood, and then the group broke up. I didn't have time to see what Gina thought of it all because a kid edged in close and said, "Ben, there's a phone call for you in the office."

Faye had come up and was talking to Gina so I went to take the call. It was Sonny and he was in a hurry. "Ben? No record on Ralph Felton—in fact, no Ralph Felton."

"Nothing at all?"

"He don't exist—at least, not in the books. Maybe he ain't got no record. Look, I gotta run. I'll see you tomorrow and we'll check with some people on the streets."

"I guess so, Sonny, catch a bass for me." I hung up and went back a little depressed. I hadn't expected anything else, but there's always the chance that it will be easy for once. Faye was bending Gina's ear, so I oozed in and took her in tow. "I guess we better get you on your way, Gina." She followed me to the door and Faye followed, talking about 200 words a minute with gusts up to 350. I know she talks to cover up loneliness, but it gets to be a problem sometimes.

Terry caught us as we were going out and said, "Good to see you, Gina. Come back when you can. Say, Ben, what do you want to do about that Percelli guy?"

I thought about it for ten seconds. "Throw his

rear out of here, Terry—tonight. See you later."

We went to the car and no sooner had Gina sat down than she said, "You're a pretty tough bird, aren't you, Delaney?" I could tell she was mad. "Faye was telling me about how scared everybody in Hot Springs is of you. And what are you kicking that kid out for? I thought you were running that place to help people?"

It was hard to explain to someone who had never been involved in a halfway house, but I wanted to try. "Look, Gina, you only have so much time. And you can only help so many kids. If you spend X number of hours on this one, why, you're taking those hours away from somebody else. And there's a few floaters like Percelli who want to hustle you. He's been in every halfway house in the country. He goes there and makes a big noise about how he's been a bad boy, but now he's seen the light and is going to be *very* good. And for awhile he is. But not really—he's got no intention of changing. Right now he's pushing drugs for a local supply, and he's even bringing it into the Vine. Now, I know at least ten kids who really want to kick the habit, and if Percelli leaves one of them can come in."

I was tired. It had been a long day. Besides, I wasn't sure I was telling the truth. Maybe Percelli *could* make it. Maybe I was giving him the final push when he needed a helping hand. I couldn't make those judgments as easily as I had a few months ago. One of the guys I put out blew his brains out the next night. I didn't like to think about that.

I guess I was all tied up in my own thoughts and

sort of forgot about Gina. Finally she said, "Well, I'm sorry. I—I guess it's pretty tough having to decide stuff like that." She looked out the window away from me. "That Faye—you think she can make it, Ben?"

"Maybe. I hope so. That's about all I can say anymore. Look, I better get you to the Club. It's nearly nine. By the way, there was nothing on Ralph Felton—but I didn't think there would be. I'll see some people tomorrow. Maybe we can turn up a name or something."

I pulled up in front of the Club and got out. I walked around and opened the door, but just as she got out someone crashed into me and shoved me to one side. I caught myself quickly and turned to see Larry Proctor take Gina by the arm. He was looking hard at me, and I knew he was jealous of his women. It was too dark for him to recognize me, but he said to Gina, "Hello, Sweetheart," then he grabbed my arm and pulled me up close, ready to rough me up.

I shoved my face up close to him and said, "Hello, Sweetheart!" He stepped back quick dropping my arm.

"Delaney!" He hated my insides, and I knew that one day he'd try to get me. Even in the darkness I could see his eyes glitter with the desire. "What are you doing here, cop?" he snarled.

"Just slumming, Proctor," I smiled brightly then ignored him and turned to Gina. "Hey, Gina, it's been a lot of fun. I'll see you tomorrow, all right?" And then I walked around and got into the car. As I drove off I could hear the argument starting, like "What are you doing with that dumb cop?" and

"I'll go with anybody I want!" and on like that. I was pleased to hear real anger in both their voices. "I have done my good deed for the day and now I am qualified for the office of Eagle Scout," I muttered. But I didn't feel like an Eagle Scout, and I lay awake a long time thinking of Gina, and Elizabeth, and George—and most of all of Elvis's thin frail face.

4

Just before dawn I heard fish breaking. I can resist anything except temptation and the sound of breaking bass, so I slipped into a pair of shorts and stepped out on the deck. Part of a moon was making a last stand in the west, and the breaking fish picked up the silver in little flashes as they rolled the mirror surface of the water. It was that special kind of cool that comes just before sunrise, and I soaked it in along with the quietness that would soon be broken by outboards all along the lake.

No need for any heavy gear for these early risers; I picked up the lightweight Garcia with a Hot Shot on it and flipped it into the boiling center of a school of breaking fish. I got a strike at once, and as always my mind goes crazy and I have a wild urge to throw down the rod and haul the fish in hand over hand. Wisdom prevailed, and I played the fish carefully, pulling it to the dock and pinching its open mouth with a thumb and forefinger.

White bass about a pound—just the right eating size. By the time the sun had routed the first fishermen out, and the Evinrude's and Merc's were sounding their *put-put-put,* punctuating the morning silences, I had four nice ones and went inside. When I bought the shack, I had planned to spend the long hours of spring fishing, but like the rest of America it was getting too crowded; now the only times I could be alone were in the middle of the night or the pink of dawn.

I cleaned the fish and stuck them in the freezer. I cooked bacon and eggs, read for awhile in a book that I didn't really understand but couldn't put down—*The Cost of Discipleship* by a German named Dietrich Bonhoeffer. Most of it was over my head, but one thing made sense; this German who was put to death by the personal order of Hitler said over and over again that there was no such thing as what he called "cheap grace." He touched a nerve there, because most of the church members I knew were not paying much for their religion. It was "cheap" in the sense that they more or less accepted the religious part of their lives on about the same terms as their clubs or lodges. Like country clubs with crosses on top. I put the book down and wondered what Bonhoeffer would have thought of the breed of evangelists that TV seemed to spawn saying with toothy grins: "Something *good* is going to happen to you!" —always with the unspoken premise, *If you will invest in my ministry!*

Old Mrs. Huitt, who lived three cabins down from me and always seemed to be up no matter how late or how early I got home, threw herself in front of my car; I stopped in time to avoid mangling her. She smiled at me through the windshield and said, "Ben, would you stop by and get me some mineral water today? I'm down to my last bottle." She picked up two five-gallon blue glass jugs and pushed them in my face, adding, "I'd go myself but I have to save on gas this week."

"OK, Helen," I said with a smile. I had heard rumors that she was rich and checked her out just from curiosity. I had been stunned to find out that she had over a million in one bank. "Anything else?"

"No. I may not be here when you get back so just put them on the front porch." She settled down with her elbows on the window, ready to give me a summary of last night's bingo game, but I nudged the gas a little and oozed out from under her. "Well, I'll see you later," she called.

I looked back through the mirror and she looked pathetic, but Hot Springs is filled with pathetic rich people. And poor people too, but the rich ones are more interesting. A lot of them are women like Helen Huitt—in their late fifties or sixties and not able or inclined to marry. Some of them hire pretty young men to squirc them around. I never know who to feel most sorry for—the trim young stud who follows these old women around—quick to light their cigarettes and careful not to look at younger women—or the old women who try desperately to buy a slice of youth and fail miserably. I wonder what they talk about? Or what they do together. Would he say, "Come on, babe, let's water ski!" or would she say, "Charles, let's go down to that new sewing center this afternoon"? It always made me think of that part of Robert Frost's poem:

Better to go down dignified
With boughten friendship by your side
Than none at all! Provide! Provide!

"Robert Frost, you were so wrong!" I snorted. I felt so pleased that I, Ben Delaney, boy philosopher, had caught the great poet in error that I made a poem myself:

Poems are made by fools like he,
But only Ben can really see!

Good thing I was a cop instead of a poet.

It was pretty quiet at the station and I was just getting ready to settle down to my reports when Jabloski stuck his bullet head inside the door and yelled at the top of his lungs: "DELANEY! THE CHIEF WANTS TO SEE YOU!" Jabloski had one pitch; he always shouted like that no matter how close he was to you. I often wondered what his courtship must have been like. He probably screamed in his wife's ear: "HOW ABOUT IT, SWEETIE, YA WANNA GET HITCHED?" alerting every ear in a square mile.

I walked past him and said, "What did you say, Tim?" He started screaming his message again. I said, "Oh, that's what I thought you said," and went into the chief's office.

Jack Ameche was sitting at his desk ignoring the forms in front of him. He looked a lot like a young Caesar Romero except he was better looking and weighed about fifty pounds more. I guess Jack looked like what I wanted to look like when I got to be fifty—but I knew I never would. He was about six feet three inches and was the same weight he had been when he played offensive tackle for the Arkansas Razorbacks—222 pounds. He had that great coloring you can't buy out of a bottle or get under a sunlamp and I always thought he came from his mother's womb with a perfect tan. As I slumped down in the chair, I noticed how he could make even a police uniform look like it came from the best store in Dallas. Everything he put on seemed to straighten up and gain importance, get more expensive somehow—just as everything I put on, no matter how much it cost, looked like it came out of a charity box. He did everything easy and if there was something he wasn't good at, it was news to me.

"Well, what's with this Williams mess?" he asked. Even his voice was too good for ordinary use; he had that perfect baritone that few announcers and most opera bassos have, and I knew that he could make himself heard a mile away—as he had done more than once in North Korea, according to Lieutenant Dempsey who had served there with Ameche.

"I don't know," I said lazily.

He looked at me, his black eyes giving off sparks, "Don't know! Well, you'd better know by tonight or you'll be walking a beat again."

"Sure, Jack."

"I mean it this time, Ben! The papers are taking the mess up, and we have to have something to throw to them—so get with it." He paused, then grinned, "Come and eat tonight. Marie said to tell you she's fixing that beef stroganoff—and banana pudding!"

"Will there be a young lady to go with it?"

Ameche grinned, his teeth snow white against the tan. "Not this time. I think she's run every filly in Hot Springs back and forth for your approval."

"Yeah, well, I'll be there by six. I can resist anything except temptation and banana pudding." It was on the tip of my tongue to tell him about the Matthews business, but the phone rang, and I left while Jack was talking to someone in a soothing voice. Probably an alderman.

I tried to get by Jabloski without rousing him, but he saw me and roared fiercely: "YOU AND DAY WILL HAVE TO COVER FOR MUNSION AND HEFLEY TODAY!"

I leaned over close to him and yelled as loud as I could: "WHY? ARE THEY SICK, TIM?" I sometimes screamed at him in self-defense, but he never noticed.

He boomed by like thunder across the bay: "NO, THEY HAD TO TESTIFY IN THAT ROBERTS CASE IN LITTLE ROCK!"

Sonny Day came in and listened to the yelling contest with a jaundiced eye. "OK, TIM, WE'LL TAKE CARE OF IT!" I bellowed. "HAVE A GOOD DAY!"

"Why do you scream at him like that?" Sonny asked disgustedly as we went into the squad room and got some coffee.

"I dunno. Maybe just to figure out if he's on the wrong pitch—or if all the rest of us are whispering."

"Well, I think you're both nuts." Sonny drank

his scalding coffee down as if it were cool lemon-ade. His real name was Sunshine Day—a fact which enrages him and the one thing for which he has never forgiven his father. I think his dad thought that a nice cheerful name might make the world brighter for what must have been one of the blackest babies ever born—but it was humiliation for my partner. In the ghetto they called him "Sunshine" until he whipped them all. Then he settled on "Sonny" and that's what most people think is on his birth certificate. I don't think any-one except me knows what his real name is. I watched him down another cup of hot coffee.

"I think you're a freak, Sunshine," I said. "Your throat must be made of iron castings and ceramic tile. I knew you darkies all got rhythm, but do all you folks have indestructible throat membranes, too?"

I could say things like this to Sonny now, but in the dim past of our relationship was one no-quarters fight that still made even my hair hurt to think of it. I had been assigned this black guy as a partner, and I tried him out with a not-very-sly racist joke the first day. He waited until the shift was over and invited me to go behind the track with him. I don't think either of us remember much about that hour, but we had to help each other to the car, and since we were not about to go to a hospital we went to his place and his mother patched us both up—without a word of rebuke. That brawl made my worst time in Nam seem like a holiday, and I guess it drained all my redneck ideas out with the blood onto the track. Right now there are two men I would trust to take care of me in the really bad spots—Ameche and Sonny.

He grinned at me and said in his clear tenor voice, "Why you messin' around with this Matthews stuff, Ben?"

I was suddenly defensive about it. "Why, Sonny, I have to look into it. He's innocent!"

"Ain't they all!"

"But, Sonny, he came right out and *admitted* to me that he didn't do it! And his very own *sister* promised that he wasn't lying."

Sonny snorted and got up to wash his cup out. "Last guilty man we had in the whole state was Tom Slaughter. And they caught him standing over two dead men with his gun smoking!"

"You know, Sonny, I've always said that Tom Slaughter was not a criminal—he was just a misunderstood youngster. I'll bet you that gun went off by accident!" I smiled brightly.

"Accident! It sure did—*six times!*"

"But that was before the days of civil rights, Officer Day." I protested as I swallowed my lukewarm coffee. "We have to have civil rights, or you won't be equal, right?"

Sonny opened his desk drawer and pulled out a cellophane-wrapped stick of jerky. He stripped the wrapping off and began to gnaw at it with gusto.

"How can you *eat* that mess? Why don't you stick to chitlins and watermelon like a decent darkie?"

"You tend to your vittles, honky, and I'll tend to mine," he said. Then he looked at me curiously. "What you into this for?"

"I got word that Matthews wanted to talk to me,

and I made the trip to Cummins. He says that he's got a fatal disease and that he made the deal with a guy named Ralph Felton to take the drop for the reward. Now, he says that Felton hasn't paid up."

"And you believe all this?" Sonny said incredulously. "I been meaning to talk to you, Ben, about the tooth fairy and all——"

"I know, I know, but you see the guy's got this kid—about six years old, and he's sick too, but there's no insurance——"

"Ben, they're gonna *fry* this guy on the 20th! What can you do about it?" Sonny was looking at me strangely as if I had just grown another set of ears.

It looked pretty grim there in that grubby squad room, and I nodded slowly. "I guess you're right, but I promised his sister-in-law that I'd check—so I guess I'll go through the motions. Not much checking to do. Will you talk to that manager of the store where the girl was killed? Just see if you can find anything out—you know, that might tell us that Matthews didn't necessarily do it."

Sonny didn't answer for a long minute, and I got uncomfortable under his stare. Then he shook his head slowly and muttered, "I knew when you got religion it would mess up your brain, Delaney. Yeah, I'll do it. What you gonna do?"

"There were two witnesses to the killing. One of them is a girl that works at the I.Q. Zoo. I guess I'll see if she can give us anything. Ask around about this gambler—not by the name of Ralph Felton. I got a feeling that's not it. But that game was in the Arlington Hotel in early October, and it was a big one. Somebody, a bellhop or a maid is bound to remember. See if you can get a line on anybody of the description, will you?"

"Yeah. And with all the gamblers in this town it ought to be simple to find one that's got no name that was in a game nearly a year ago! Guess you better start *praying* about this—because I don't think no *natural* methods will work." He grinned at me slyly as he always did when he mentioned my "getting religion." It was still a matter of humor to him, as it was to just about everybody else in the department. And sometimes even to me.

It was after twelve when I pulled in front of the club where Gina worked and went inside. It was dark as it always is in these dives, and I stood still for a minute waiting for my eyes to get accustomed to the dim lights. Somebody said, "Hello, Delaney," and I made out Wash Buford standing beside me. We'd had a little trouble in the past and I was no favorite of Wash's, but he's about average for one of the creeps that owned these dives. His voice was raspy, and he had a whisper he'd picked up in prison. "Lookin' for someone?"

My eyes had gotten used to the dark and I saw Gina sitting at a table with some guy. "I'll send for you if I need you, Wash." He glared at me, then backed away, disappearing into the smoky darkness.

I guess there may be a sadder sight somewhere than the scenes that roll on endlessly inside these small bars all over the country, but offhand I can't think of any. Huddling in the darkness, there they are, the misplaced persons of our emotional culture. The bunnies are ravenous for romance, yet settle for what they call "making out." The futile, acne-pitted men drift out of high school into a world so surfeited with unskilled labor there is a competition for the sacking jobs at Safeway. Somewhere they must have had at least a hope that if you are sunny, cheery, sincere, group-adjusting, and popular, the world is yours, a world of barbecue pits, diaper-service, percale sheets, friends for dinner, and the home projector. But it all gets lost or sidetracked into a den like this—a murky cave filled with losers. I've read about underground rivers where the fish lose their eyes, trapped so far from light, and I never step into one of these bars without thinking that somehow I've stepped into some sort of murky cavern far away from all that's good and wholesome—so far away that those who grope in the watery darkness have lost all traces of a moral vision.

I navigated the crowded floor and stood over Gina and the guy sitting with her. She glanced up and a look of alarm swept across her face, and she looked around quickly to see who was watching.

"Gina, I have to see you," I said, then looked at the man she was with. He was some sort of small-time businessman, probably trying to convince himself he was Humphrey Bogart chatting with Ingrid Bergman about love and life. "You don't mind too much, do you, Gerald?" I asked, and he did his world-famous disappearing act so neatly that it was about ready to take on the road. I slipped into his chair.

"What—what do you want, Delaney?" She was nervous—probably about what Wash would think of her having fellowship with the fuzz.

"We have to make a call, Gina. You have a coat?"

"I can't leave *now!*" she said in a whisper.

"Never think negative thoughts, Gina." I yawned and got up, pulling her to her feet and starting toward the door with her in tow. "The power of positive thinking is a wonderful thing." She was stuttering and trying to hang back, but we got to the door and there was Wash waiting with a look of hatred jumping out of his eyes.

"Something wrong, Gina?" he asked. He wanted to swing on me like crazy, but he knew I had the edge. In a dark alley it would have been different.

"Wash, Miss Romero and I have just heard of a wonderful new print they have up at Mason's Gallery. It's an 18th century watercolor by one of the most neglected artists of his age. It's imperative that we get our bid in before the big buyers snap it up. All right with you, Wash?"

His eyes glowed piggishly in the dark and he whispered, "Sure, Delaney, you just have fun. One of these days we'll talk about it—when you ain't wearing that shield."

"But didn't you know, Wash, I wear it all the time—even in the shower and pinned to my jammies."

I pulled Gina outside and we blinked in the light of day, then I shoved her into the car. We got under way and she said, "I can lose my job for a thing like this!"

"I bleed, sweetie." The streets were almost empty, and there was total silence until we pulled up in front of First National. "I hope you got the key to that box," I said as I opened the door.

"Yes, I have it," she said grimly. Her back was straight as a ruler as we went in. We did the business with getting someone else in with a key, and they wanted me to wait outside, so I did. She came out clutching the envelope nervously and we left the bank.

"Let's get some coffee," I said and she followed me into a grubby restaurant. We sat down on the cracked plastic seats and Gina said, "I'm afraid to open it, Ben!" She was breathing in short gasps and perspiration lay on her full upper lip. "Do you think it will help George?"

"Open it and we'll see."

She slit the envelope and took out a single sheet of paper, then looked at it. She turned it over and then looked up, her eyes bright with shock. "Ben! It's—it's *blank!* There isn't anything on it!"

I sipped the coffee, wondering how they had managed to make it so bad. Then I glanced at the paper she held out to me, not feeling anything much.

"Why, you're not even surprised!" Gina said angrily.

"Not much. Look, the bird that thought all this up is a pretty sharp cat. He's a gambler and a pretty good one, I'd say. It wouldn't be any trick for him to switch a real confession right before George's eyes. Even if it were here it wouldn't mean much. It wouldn't be his real name."

"But—it's not *fair!*" Gina said with a painful sob in her voice.

"Honey, it never was." I said softly, taking her hand. "Look, don't get shook up. I didn't think this would amount to anything, but we have to take every shot. Now, can you go to see George tomorrow and tell him about this?"

"What for? What good can it do?"

"None, maybe, but it may make him mad enough to remember something new. And we've got to have something, Gina. Time's awastin'."

"Oh, all right, I'll go" she said in a tired voice and somehow the strength had drained out of her. She sipped at the coffee listlessly, and I saw that she had quit. "I guess I ought to get back."

I looked at my watch. "Yeah, me too." An impulse struck me. "Look, what time can you get out of that—place?" I asked.

"About six tonight. Why?"

"I'm going to eat with some friends of mine about seven. Why don't you come along? Good cooking."

"With you?" she said quickly. She shook her head and got up to go, then she stopped and looked off for a minute, then turned and there was a funny light in her eyes as if she were enjoying some sort of private joke. "You mean it, Delaney? Pick me up at six-thirty."

I took her back and let her out at the club and she walked in without another word. For the rest of my shift I stopped from time to time wondering what the chief of police and his sweet wife would say when I brought a barmaid to their home for supper.

It was nearly seven-thirty by the time we pulled the Galaxie up in front of the Ameche's classy lakeshore home. It was a big place built of native stone and cypress. There were some fat pillars out in front and the circular drive contained a Jag, a jeep, and a new motor home big enough to retire in. As we got out and walked up the marble steps, Gina looked at me peculiarly and said in a whisper, "I suppose this is the Mafia, right?"

I reached out to press the bell, but the door opened and Marie Ameche threw her arms around me as usual with the kissing bit. "Hey, Marie, watch it!" I said as I untangled her arms. "Your husband may be around."

"You never worried about a husband in your life, Delaney," Marie said. She was, I guess, the best looking woman I'd ever seen. She was fifty-one and looked thirty. She was some kind of Indian, and I guess she disproved for me all the dumb stories about dumpy squaws, because she was a couple of inches over five feet and didn't weigh more than 110. They told me in hushed voices that even when she was pregnant you could never tell from the back; she stayed so trim. She had the flawless skin of a model and moved like a ballerina. Now she looked with her dark eyes at Gina and I would like to have read her thoughts, but nobody can do that with an Indian.

"I'm Marie Ameche," she smiled and suddenly leaned forward and kissed Gina on the cheek lightly. Gina was taken aback and though she opened her mouth, Marie's striking beauty and kiss robbed her of speech.

"This is Gina Romero, Marie. A friend of mine."

"Well, she's in bad company." Jack suddenly appeared and stood with his arm around Marie looking more and more like a Latin matinee idol. He was smiling down at Gina, and I could see he liked her.

"Well, are we gonna eat or not?" I said quickly. They hustled us inside and soon Marie had disappeared with Gina to put the finishing touches on the food, so she said, and Jack took me into the study to show me the new rifle he'd just bought.

His study was lined in English walnut and the walls were covered with guns of all kinds—all except *cheap* kinds, that is. Pistols, shotguns, deer rifles, muzzle-loaders, you name it, and Jack had it.

He took a rifle from a cloth laid across his desk and handed it to me. It was a new Browning shotgun. "How do you like it?" he asked eagerly.

"How much did it cost?" I asked. I could never figure out how Jack could buy all these guns—not to mention the fancy cars, the townhouse, and the good schools for the kids. Somebody had said that his wife had money, and I guess that had to be it.

"I practically stole it from Vince Whittington. Only paid five hundred for it—and I could get seven right now."

I handed the gun back and said, "Good-looking piece, Jack."

He sat down and began to sight the gun, and we talked about hunting and how we'd have to get back to Texas for a deer this year for sure. While he was sighting the gun, I studied him, thinking about how little I knew about him and how hard it was to explain how I trusted him so much. Oh, everybody knew he had been an All-American at

Arkansas and that he had a drawer full of medals from the Korean affair. He had been a hotshot detective on the Los Angeles Police Force for a time, then had come to Hot Springs and settled down for life. I never could understand how he could take that step down—but I heard once that Marie didn't think Los Angeles was the place to raise a family, so they had settled in Hot Springs. All I knew was if I were in the worst spot in the world this was the man I wanted watching my back. Marie called from the dining room, "Come on you two," and we seated ourselves at the massive oval table that came from Holland. It was one of those meals where the food and the eating were good. Sometimes that's not so; I've been at a few meals where the food was excellent but for whatever reason the ceremony of it was wrong and the meal would sit like a dead armadillo in your belly. The Italians had the right idea, I decided. While new home builders were building the family room to eat in—or else tacking on the dining room to a section of the living room, every Italian I knew built a large, comfortable dining room that served a real purpose. The meals were not something you did to get from one part of existence to another; they were ceremony, and a time for living together. No hurrying through the quick frozen fish or pasty instant potatoes in order to get somewhere. It was a time for talk, for sharing, and as we sat around the table through the tasty beef stroganoff and the crispy salad, the banana pudding and coffee, I looked over at Gina and saw that she was at ease and could chat with Jack and Marie as if she had known them for years.

"Let's go sit on the deck," Jack said, and we got heavily to our feet and made our way to the redwood deck that extended over the water. We sat there in the warm darkness and another miracle took place; we didn't have to *talk* for long periods, but just sat quietly watching the moonlight on the lake, the stars glimmering overhead, and listening to the nighthawks and the owls talk to each other. It was the sort of time that only people who trust each other can have; it's strangers who need conversation.

We stayed for an hour, and then I got up and said, "We have to go, folks."

"Oh, not yet," Marie said.

"It's past my bedtime," I grinned, helping Gina out of the deep chair she had almost gone to sleep in. We went to the door and Marie said, "Gina, make him bring you back, hear? Or maybe you can come some afternoon and we can go shopping or something."

"I'd like that," Gina said softly. "It's been such a good evening."

We said our good-nights and got into the car. I started back to town to drop Gina off, and she didn't say a word until we were almost there.

"They're nice!" she said.

"They liked you. I could tell."

"I guess you take a lot of girls there, huh?"

"A constant stream." I didn't tell her that they usually had a prospective girlfriend there for me.

"They're rich, aren't they?" she mused. "What does he do?"

I turned to glance at her. "He's a policeman." I grinned to see her almost jump with surprise.

"Matter of fact, he's my boss. Chief of police."

She didn't answer again until I pulled up in front of the house and led her to the door. She was deep in thought; the smooth furrows of her forehead had tiny wrinkles, and she said, "Well, they're nice anyway—" she paused and gave me a gamine smile, "I guess some cops *are* nice."

"We're cute as anything," I said. Her perfume was not strong but enough to faintly remind you of her dark attractiveness. We looked at each other suddenly in the way that a man and a woman will sometimes, and I heard the night singing clearly, and beyond that, her breathing quickened, as did my own. With an effort I directed my mind to business: "Try to get what you can out of George. Take this tape recorder and go over it as best you can."

"All right. When do you want it?" She sounded angry and I didn't know why.

"I'll pick it up tomorrow night." I didn't know how to leave, so I just said, "See you tomorrow, Gina," and plunged off the porch quickly. As I pulled out she was standing under the dim light watching me go, and for a long time that night I lay awake thinking of the evening and I couldn't help comparing her with Ann. They looked nothing alike, but there was something about the cocktail waitress that brought back memories of my dead wife that stabbed at me like knives, and I knew that I had been kidding myself—the old saying, "Time heals all wounds," is just garbage.

Saturday is a bad day for cops.

So is Monday, Tuesday. . . . But on Saturday it's impossible to avoid the thought that people who lead normal lives are home doing those useless, lovely things that have absolutely no redeeming social value, like watching college football, raking leaves, popping popcorn, and reading old copies of the *Congressional Record*.

Policemen work on Saturdays just like murderers, rapists, burglars—oh, all of us in the trade.

As Sergeant Friday once said, "I was working the day watch out of homicide." It sounds thrilling enough, but it means I was typing out overdue reports on an old Royal used by Eddie Poe to dash off *The Fall of the House of Usher* and other assorted psychopathic fiction.

Cops eventually arrive at a strange mindset which leads them to be absolutely positive that *everything* they experience will (sooner or later) re-

quire testimony that will stand up in court. This is
a result of over-testifying—an occupational haz-
ard for all police officers. Time after time the
officer must take the stand and testify to the integ-
rity of the evidence that will either strap the defendant to the chair or set him free. He learns quickly
to forget that he has opinions; the court is not
interested in such fragile human emotions. It is
only those things which can be weighed, photo-
graphed, analyzed, tagged, measured, and firmly
fixed that the court will admit as evidence; and the
prudent officer will be prone to close his mind to
any element less concrete than the material that
will fit on a report to the Chief of Detectives.

The report that I was working on was simple
enough in those terms.

NAME: Anthony Pappas
ADDRESS: 106 Vine Street
AGE: 15
CHARGE: Homicide
DETAILS: Subject fired a .240 grain slug from a
    .44 Magnum into the heart of Leon Rogers.

That was the clinical evidence.

What I *wanted* to write on the report was that
Tony Pappas (age fifteen) shot a no-good alcoholic
deviate (with an impressive record for several nas-
ty offenses) for attempting to rape his eleven-year-
old sister. Personally I felt that the defendant
deserved a commendation for preserving his little
sister from Rogers who was, from all reports, a
mixture of Adolf Hiter, Dracula, and Uriah Heep.
But all I dared put down was the time, date, man-

ner, and cause of Leon Rogers' departure for that undiscovered country from whose bourn no traveler returns.

Sonny came into the squad room as I was filling out reports and said with an Afro-American leer, "Guess who dropped a dime on Matthews?"

"Annette Funicello?"

"Close! But seriously folks. . . ."

"I give up."

"Bernie Floyd! Ain't *that* a kick in the head?"

It was. Bernie Floyd was a denizen of the Hot Springs underworld, but not a card-carrying hood. He was one of those nebulous characters who couldn't really decide if they were real criminals or just plastic imitations. Bernie was a flashy dresser and did unintentional imitations of Bogart and Cagney from the old Warner Brothers prison movies. But Bernie hadn't pulled a trigger yet—not that I knew of. He was in training for it, and I was sure that he'd go over the edge one day, but up to now he was just a punk. Dan Duryea used to play this role better than anybody.

"How does that grab you?" Sonny asked with a smile like the grill of a '57 Chrysler.

"I like it, Sonny. It fits so well there *must* be something wrong. Where is Brother Bernie right now?"

"I would guess he is using his reward money only to get coked to the gills," Sonny said. He threaded a report blank into a machine and began pecking out his own reports with remarkable apathy. "The pushers will be filled with joy that one of their own has *arrived.*"

"Has Floyd started sampling his wares?" I asked.

75

We had known for some time that Bernie was dealing in a minor way, but the drug problem had ballooned so enormously in Hot Springs that we had to concentrate on the big score; there were a hundred minor pushers like Floyd and if we started chasing them, we'd never get the big boys.

"Don't they all—sooner or later?" Sonny typed in a smooth rhythm unlike my own chopping, but he paused long enough to look sideways at me and add, "He's holed up at the Holiday Inn if you want to rake him over."

"Living pretty high," I mused. "Guess I'll go over for the afternoon tea."

"Maybe he's telling the truth. Maybe he really did see Matthews blast the girl. At least he convinced enough people to collect the reward."

"Maybe interest rates will go down."

"Maybe you're emotionally involved." Sonny suggested. He looked at me with what he thought was a supercilious smirk.

"Are you giving me a supercilious smirk?" I demanded.

"Betcha bird!" he nodded, and went back to his reports.

I filled out all my reports, then ran out all the possible leads on the seventeen cases I was assigned before I took a run to the Holiday Inn to check out Floyd's story. I see a lot of TV detectives and read most of the books, and it gives me a real laugh to see how they all drop everything to concentrate on one case. Ameche would love it if I did that!

But finally I made it to the Holiday Inn and asked the clerk the number of Floyd's room.

The room clerk had eyes the color of spit and respect only for those who required a CPA to figure their taxes; I didn't qualify, so he said in his best imitation of Sir Cedric Hardwicke, "Ah—Mr. Floyd occupies Suite 9A."

"Thanks, Jack," I nodded cheerfully. "I'll remember you in my will." He was not impressed.

I went up in the Otis and pushed the button marked 9A. It was a long wait, but finally Bernie himself opened the heavy door. He was wearing a sickly green velour robe and an expression to match. "Whatcha want, Delaney?" he asked through his adenoids.

"You're not glad to see me, Bernie. I can tell." I brushed past him and sat down on a useless-looking chair as if I had settled in for the long winter night.

The room was semi-opulent, with a facade of expensive gilt that hid the raw bones of lath and lumber. Pseudo-Grecian plastic tile concealed the sprinkler system, the wiring, and the insulation overhead. The walls were four by eight sheets of Weyerhauser Paneling #232 Spanish Oak, and the floor was Pattern 16C Honey Beige. Imitation eighteenth-century chandeliers with 60-watt Westinghouse bulbs gave off enough light to read by, and nowhere could a trace of *real* craftsmanship be found. All plastic-made in a mold for plastic Americans who have long forgotten the thrill of a made-by-human-hand artifact.

"Bernie," I said, "leave us talk."

"I got nothing to talk to you about, cop. You got a warrant?"

"What we have here," I explained patiently, "is a

failure to communicate." I got up from the chair and walked over to Floyd, taking him by the lapels of his unfortunate green robe and lifting him off the floor in my finest Bogart manner. His eyes grew big (except for the pupils) and he began to sputter. "I got rights!" he said.

"You have *problems,* not rights, Bernie." I nodded toward the door to his bedroom and added, "I strongly suspect that you have a woman in that room!"

"So what?" he demanded. "That ain't against the law!"

"No, but I suspect also that if I looked hard enough I would find *drugs* in there." I shook my head like a disapproving high school principal. "Drugs, Bernie, and if I do, you know what a drag that will be! Just one ounce of Colombian—and you're in Cummins. One to five for possession! It's really not worth it."

Bernie cast a nervous glance at the bedroom door, then began to bargain with me.

"Ah, Delaney, a little grass—what the hell? Why, you could find fifty high school kids with more than that—and no hard stuff—I swear!"

"True," I admitted, "and I will promise to leave your premises with no bust"—I smiled at him with all my might—"if you will tell me who you split the money with from the Matthews payoff. Who paid you to set him up?"

If I had not been sure before, I was then. Cops spend a vast amount of time reading faces, trying to decide if people are honest or not. By long practice they get very good at spotting a lie.

A good musician will hear an off-key note that

most people miss, and a real artist will see a half-tone in a watercolor that makes his teeth grind. A garden variety detective will see the tiny twitch of a lip or the microscopic beat of an eye that most would ignore—but to the real cop it screams "LIE!" in letters a foot high.

So, when Bernie said hastily, "The Matthews case! Delaney, I swear I told the straight goods!" I knew he was lying like a car salesman.

I knew he was lying; he knew he was lying. The problem was, how do we arrive at the truth? Time was of the essence, as they say, so I eased the leather sap (with the six-ounce lead weight sewn securely in the tip) out of my back pocket and said with the saddest expression I could muster: "Bernie, you got a death wish or what?"

"Honest, Delaney," he began to beg, "there ain't no *profit* in lying to you!" This was as close to a sacred oath as Bernie could get, and he whipped out a tan silk handkerchief, wiped his brow, and said rapidly, "It was just a break, I tell you! Me and Matthews wasn't close, but we got drunk together maybe once a month, and we bowled sometimes. Well, he was pretty well lit and he told me, see? About the holdup, you know? Well, I thought he was just blowin' off, but then I see the papers and they told it just like he said."

"So you did your duty as a citizen, right?"

"Yeah, that's right."

"When?"

"Whattya mean *when?*"

"You didn't go soon as Matthews told you. You waited until you found out about the reward, didn't you, Bernie?"

"Well—I didn't wanna blow the whistle—but I seen it was my duty."

I slapped the blackjack into my hand and went to stand beside Floyd. I am only five ten, but I weigh 190. My face is very stern, as Sonny says, and when I am serious or angry there is usually a sudden urge for the people I am questioning to start cooperating.

So my face made people nervous, but that was all right sometimes. All I had to do was keep hitting my big hand with the leaded sap, look at them with my serious expression, and pretty soon folks would be more *helpful*.

But not Bernie Floyd. I only carried the sap for visual-aid purposes and would never use it. But I had Bernie fooled, and he claimed for nearly twenty minutes that he had heard Matthews confess to the killing.

Finally I decided my infallible sense of discernment was fallible. "OK, Floyd. I'll want to talk to you again. Don't leave town." I walked to the bedroom door and opened it. A scared-looking girl about seventeen years old looked at me in panic, and she backed away from me so suddenly that the hollywood bed caught her just behind the knees and she sat down suddenly.

I gave her my best smile and said, "I have to run along now, Stella, but I'll be back before you know it. When you go, don't look back."

I left the hotel and called Gina. Elizabeth said she had taken Elvis to the Western Sizzlin. I beat it over there and got a steak while waiting for them. The sirloin tips were the special, $2.95 with a baked potato. I ate hungrily, and just as I was finishing I saw Gina come in leading Elvis by the hand. They ordered and came by my table with their trays.

"Hey, here's two places," I called.

Gina spotted me and hesitated, but Elvis slipped into the seat across from me and said, "Hi."

He was wearing a blue polo shirt. His jeans were new and stiff, and his tennis shoes were old and limp. He looked at me with those big brown eyes so long I finally looked away. My boy had been like that. He had looked at people straight as a laser, formed his judgment, and it had been an unerring sort of thing.

"Where you been?" I asked as Gina finally sat down.

"Oh, just to a movie," she said. "Elvis wanted to see it and Anna didn't feel like going."

Elvis launched into a full-scale description of the film. It lasted through the salad. Then he abruptly asked, "Can I go to the bathroom, Aunt Gina?"

The sudden transition caught her off guard, but Gina quickly said, "Sure, you go right over to that door, Elvis. Hurry, now."

As the boy disappeared I asked, "What does he say about his father?"

Gina seemed nervous. She pushed the napkin on her tray from one position to another. "Nothing," she said. Then she looked right at me. "Well, not really. Look, Delaney, I—I guess I did wrong. The boy thinks that you're—"

"That I'm going to get his father off Death Row?" I finished angrily. "I *told* you not to do that!"

"Well what can I tell him! That his daddy's go-

81

ing to burn?" Her eyes flashed angrily, but they were blurred with sudden tears. "I didn't tell him you could do it. He's—he's so smart!" she moaned. Then the waitress brought their hamburgers and she forced herself to be calm.

"Are you saying it's hopeless?" she demanded when the waitress left.

"I'm saying Matthews has got about as much chance of being pardoned as I have of being elected Pope!"

"But if he's innocent. . . ?"

"That's not enough, Sweetheart," I said grimly. "The D.A. needs a conviction in order to get re-elected. The governor needs a conviction because he rode into office on a 'get tough on criminals' promise. The press needs a conviction because it sells more papers. Anyway, he doesn't have a support group."

"What's that?"

I leaned back and looked at her youthful face which still had some hope in it. "Gina," I said gently, "if George were a cause, he'd have a chance. If he were rich, he could shop around for judges and politicians. If he were a queer or a spic, maybe, the Civil Liberties Union would go to bat for him. But he's not any of those, so he'll just go down the old porcelain ornament next week."

Gina looked startled. Her innocence was, to some degree, intact, and she was still waiting for right to triumph. "But it's not that way, is it, Ben?"

It was the first time she had called me by my first name. I felt good about it, but it was a blind alley. Elvis had surfaced from the bathroom and settled himself by Gina. "Boy, I'm hungry!" he said, and reached for his hamburger.

"Wait a minute," Gina said, She looked directly at me, a glint in her eyes, and said, "Sergeant Delaney is a religious man, Elvis. Maybe he'd like to say a prayer."

"OK," Elvis piped up, "go ahead."

My face was burning, and I knew that the girl was trying to get to me, and I knew she had chosen a good way. Public prayers give me trouble. I have some problem with prayer in general but I'd heard so many "canned" prayers—obvious pieces of rhetoric for public performance—that I didn't feel comfortable with it.

Once I had gone to visit a church in Arkadelphia with some friends of mine, a married couple. Well, they got into a fuss like I used to do with Ann before she died. Nothing serious, you know, but it was white-lip time for an hour.

We went inside and the pastor saw Jim and called on him to "lead in prayer." I hadn't been a Christian too long, and I expected Jim to say, "Sorry, I can't pray for a little while . . . get someone else." Instead he said the most eloquent prayer I'd ever heard. Then, on the way back to Hot Springs, they took up arms against each other like it was World War III.

I couldn't figure it out. Still can't.

And what about "blessings" over food? It's fine in the dining room at home—but what if you're with a hard-nosed bunch of flatfeet at Coy's Steak House? Do you tell them all to shutup because you want to say grace?

Finally I looked hard at Gina and said, "Last week I ate at the cafeteria at Ouachita Baptist University at Arkadelphia. Went over to speak to a sociology class. Most everyone there bowed their heads for a silent prayer before they ate. The guy I was with saw me watching, I guess, and he grinned and said, 'Just bow your head and count to ten if you feel pressure.' I knew what he meant. *There* you were out of place if you didn't say grace. *Here,* you're a freak if you do."

Gina said, "Oh—well, if you don't want to. . . ."

"Let *me* say it," Elvis piped up. "I'm the best pray-er in my whole Sunday school." Without any sign of embarrassment he bowed his head and said in a very normal tone, as if God were sitting down to lunch with us, "Thank you, God, for the hamburgers and cokes—and please let my daddy come home soon. In Jesus' name. Amen!"

I looked across at Gina. Her eyes had a glisten and those hard lines that were just beginning to touch her mouth were dissolved. She reached over and hugged Elvis, saying, "Amen!"

Elvis was fascinated by policemen as everyone is, and he asked about thirty questions a minute between—and during—mouthfuls. He finally got down to where did I live and personal stuff.

"Are you married?"

"Not now." I felt Gina's eyes fasten on me.

"I guess you don't have any kids, huh?"

It was still hard for me to talk about Scott, but I made myself smile and say, "I had a boy. He'd be about your age—if he'd lived."

Kids are the only realists. When they want to know, they ask. Damn the torpedoes, Gridley.

"What did he die of?" Elvis asked.

"He—was in an accident. And his mother."

"Elvis, finish your chips." Gina had seen I couldn't handle it, so she hurried the boy along. She got up and said, "You don't know any reliable babysitters, do you, Ben?"

"For Elvis?"

"Yes. I've got to . . ." she stopped and glanced at him, then got some change from her purse. "Get me some gum will you, Sweetie? Get two packages of spearmint." She watched him gallop off and said hurriedly. "I've got to take Anna to see George tomorrow. She doesn't want Elvis to go. But I don't know anyone to leave him with."

"Well—if you'd trust the fuzz, I'm off tomorrow."

She gave me an odd look. "You sure?"

"Sure I'm sure! What time you leaving?"

"About nine in the morning. We should be back by four in the afternoon."

"I'll see you at nine."

I paid my check and left in a hurry.

Gina had seen through me like I had plate glass over my chest. Since Scott was killed I hadn't been able to be around kids very long at a time. It hurt too much. Now I was wondering if I was setting myself up for another kick in the teeth.

Old Roger Bacon knew about it: *He that hath wife and children hath given hostages to fortune.* And when I lost Ann and Scott I went out and bought the biggest lock I could find and locked whatever

door it is that people use to get inside us. I locked
the door, threw the key away, and nailed a big sign
on it.

KEEP OUT!
NO TRESPASSERS!
NOBODY ALLOWED INSIDE
BEN DELANEY!

But it was a sorry way to live.

I went home and watched a Marx Brothers Film Festival after I left Gina and Elvis. I couldn't sleep until very early in the morning, then just as I was drifting off, a car stopped outside, quickly followed by a thunderous banging on the door.

I staggered across the room and opened it, staring blankly at Sonny. He had his fishing clothes on and looked surprised to see that I wasn't dressed.

"You weren't up yet," he said.

"Oh, sure. I just wear these pajamas to save my good clothes." I stomped back to the bed saying, "Boat's ready. Better fill it up if you go far."

"Hey, Ben, I maybe got a line on the Matthews bit." He went to my rod case and picked out my best Garcia. "Guess I'll use this one."

"Need anything else? How you fixed for socks and underwear?"

"I'll let you know," Sonny grinned, then he looked puzzled. "I nosed around a little and got zero, but last night one of my informers calls me—a little bean eater named Juan Martino. He acts like he's got the secret of the ages. I have to go meet him out at Gulpha Gorge and we play hide-and-seek for an hour. I think he's read too many bad spy stories. Anyway, when I finally promise on the grave of George Washington Carver to keep him out of it, he says he *maybe* knows something about this gambler we're looking for."

"All *right!*" I said. "Yes, Virginia, there is a Santa Claus!"

Sonny held up his meaty hand. "Wait, now, he didn't know much. He said he remembers the game because he filled in for his brother-in-law who had measles. He was a bellhop at the Arlington, you know? He remembers the game 'cause that's about all he did—wait on the gamblers. And he made the guy Matthews described; that's pretty sure."

"Did he have a name for us?"

"Naw, nothing that good. You wanna talk to him yourself, here's the number. He's nervous, so don't spook him." He turned and headed for the dock where I kept the boat, but stopped at the door. "One thing he did tell me, Ben, and it'll curl your hair."

"I always wanted curly hair."

"Juan said he didn't know your man—but he made somebody else that was in the game." Sonny grinned like a shark and said, "Vito Lamotta."

"Don Vito!" I said in surprise.

"So Juan says—and he's seen Vito a time or two."

"Well, maybe I better go ask Lamotta about this guy."

Sonny looked at me with compassion. "Ask a Mafia Don for help? No, wait 'til you hear my plan!"

"Let me hear your plan."

"We will stand out in front of the Arlington Hotel and ask every person who passes, 'Do you know the name of a gambler who was in a card game at this hotel a year ago?' "

I thought it over as I began buttering Texas toast. "It'll never fly, but wait 'til you hear my plan."

"What is your plan?"

"Your mission, Mr. Phelps, should you choose to accept it, will be to get everything you can from those eyewitnesses. I'll take care of Don Vito."

"Well, you've had a pretty full life, boy," Sonny said, grinning, "and your ticket to glory is all punched, so if you wanna mess around with Mafia types you just fly right at it. I'm going fishing."

I fixed some toast and coffee while Sonny rattled around getting the boat ready. By the time I had the eggs slizzling in the skillet I heard the Black Max burst into a roar and then Sonny tore out of the slip like he always does—full throttle.

While I ate breakfast, I thought about Vito Lamotta. He had been big in the numbers in New York, and I'd heard he could give a guy ulcers with a look. No one ever knows about the Mafia, but Lamotta must have been pretty powerful to cut out the way he did. Most Dons in that outfit are "retired" with a bullet in the brain, but about five years ago Lamotta walked away from it, bought a castle on the lake here, and kept a low profile. He wasn't too active in any of the local criminal activities—I guess Hot Springs looked pretty small to him after New York. But I'd heard enough to figure out that he wasn't completely retired, so I made up my mind to make a call later that day.

I wasn't supposed to pick Elvis up until nine, so I read for a couple of hours. Terry had given me a new Bible for my birthday, something called the Amplified Version. "It's written for retarded police officers." Terry had grinned when he gave it to me.

I had always liked to read, but I'd never opened a Bible until a year before. Then I started in on the first page determined to read it straight through. I did pretty well for awhile, but when I got to all the "begats," I bogged down and went visiting the sections that appealed to me. I liked the parts in red best—the words of Jesus—and I just about wore the Gospels out. The letters of Paul were so difficult that I had to work at the meaning like it was an algebra problem. As for the last book, Revelation, well . . . I felt like my drinking Uncle George. He was a big coon hunter, and one of his dogs he named Revelation. I asked him why once, and he looked at me with a twinkle and said, "I named him Revelation 'cause I don't understand a thing about him!"

But *one* part of the Bible I understood, or thought I did, and that was the Psalms.

When I first started reading them I thought they were pretty boring, but as I kept on I saw something else: this David was high on Jehovah! He just couldn't be still a minute and insisted that everybody join him. "Let *us* praise the Lord!" he kept on saying. "Let everything that hath breath praise the Lord!"

I got to reading in the old Bible about David, and in one place it tells how he got so excited he *danced* before the Lord! I'd like to have seen that! That Jew jumping and singing with all his might! Don't guess King David would be too welcome in lots of churches today. I've about decided, after seeing quite a few of God's frozen people, it would be a lot easier to restrain a fanatic than to resurrect a corpse!

Anyway, I read a bunch of the Psalms and then I got dressed and went down to pick Elvis up. He was waiting on the front porch when I pulled up; then Gina and Anna came out all dressed up.

"You sure it'll be OK?" Gina asked.

"I can guarantee it. Call me at this number when you get back."

"All right. You want me to tell George anything?"

"If you could get anything new it might help, but I think he's told us all he knows. I've got a very small lead that I'm checking out—but don't even mention it."

"I'll call soon as we get back. Bye now, Elvis. You mind Mr. Delaney, you hear?" She kissed him and got into the Camaro with Elizabeth.

Elvis waved until they went around the corner, then he said, "You want to play checkers?"

"Sure, but later. We got to go to church first, then we eat, then I beat your tail at checkers."

"I betcha don't," he said. "Where're we going to church?"

"Well, it's not really a church, but it's a place I have to sort of look after. You remember the place where we first met? Called the Vine?"

"Oh, sure, I remember," he nodded. "Can we eat at the Taco Mexito after church?"

"Yeah, sure," I agreed. It was not my favorite place but at least the Health Department hadn't found evidence to close it down. Oh, well, I read in the New Testament once that the first disciples were promised that if they ate any deadly thing it wouldn't kill them. Thinking of the tacos they served I hoped folks today were still under warranty.

"Do I call you Mr. Delaney or Sergeant Delaney like on *Dragnet*?" Elvis asked when we were headed north on Central.

"Well, when we're with people, I guess either one will do. When it's just us, call me Ben."

He thought it over for a brief time; he did that quite a lot. Made me think of Scott. Elvis was so much like Scott—the same slow grin, the way he thought things over like an old man, the way he curled his feet under him when he sat down—he brought Scott back to me so clearly! But this time it was without the old gut-wrenching pain. Elvis wasn't Scott, but somehow he had given me my son again. Now I watched as he chewed over what I'd said.

"OK," he agreed. "Do you take your gun to church?"

"Well, yes." Kids could really get me on a guilt trip. *Who would I shoot at church?* I wondered suddenly. *Would it be worse to shoot someone in church than out of church?* I gave up.

I knew he wanted to see the gun. All kids do. I unleathered it, checked the safety, and held it down on the seat where he could see it.

He looked at the gun for a long time then blasted me with another of his questions—the one everybody wants to ask but only small kids dare. "Did you ever shoot anyone?"

"Yes."

"Did they die?"

"Two of them did." I hurried on to explain to him, "They both came at me out of an alley, and both of them had guns and were trying to kill me."

And one of them was only seventeen years old, I *didn't* say. The older one was blasting away at me with a Saturday Night Special. He missed me three times before I got off a shot that dropped him. I *thought* the other one was shooting, I'm pretty sure he aimed his gun at me, but after I put him down and we checked the guns, the .22 he'd been carrying had a full load. The kid hadn't fired a shot. But I had.

There's a lot of gamey things in my book I wish I could erase, but this was the one that woke me up lots of nights. No matter how bad I felt about it or how much I confessed it, every time I thought of the kid, it was like getting an ingrown toenail mashed. Terry said once that I wasn't as ready to forgive as God, because God had forgiven me, but *I* hadn't.

Elvis had been thinking it over so long I was startled when he said, "I'm glad they didn't kill you, Ben." He moved a little closer on the seat to me and added, "It wasn't your fault."

We parked the Galaxie and went into the Vine where the guys had already set up for the morning service. Terry looked up as we came in. "Who's your buddy, Ben?" he asked.

"Elvis Matthews is my good buddy. This is Terry." They took their time looking each other over. Terry didn't make the mistake a lot of grown-ups make of rushing a kid. He smiled and let the boy make the first move.

Finally Elvis smiled and said, "Hi," and Terry was admitted to his club.

"Let's go to the office for a few minutes," Terry said. "We have about ten minutes before the service starts."

I followed him and Elvis stuck close to me. There were several papers on the desk and Terry nodded toward them. "You need to sign all those," and while I signed he filled me in on things. Terry really ran the place; I was just a paper-signer. He rattled off progress reports on kids at the Vine; who was clean and who had taken a fall. All routine until he said, "One more thing—you won't like it."

I said, "You wanna see a list of things I don't like?"

"Faye's split." He saw I was unhappy and added, "Oh, she's still in town, and her things are still in her room, Tanya says, but she didn't come in for two nights—and you know what that means."

I knew all right. These kids were tightrope walkers—every step was a maybe for them. They oozed into drugs so easy, some of them getting their basic training from parents already hooked, and lots of them getting started in elementary schools. The pushers had worked like beavers from college to high school, middle school, and then elementary. Next they'd invade the day-care centers.

Easy to get on, almost impossible to get off. The very best federal program for addicts is at Lexington, and their most optimistic claim is that they *help* one percent.

Faye would have plenty of encouragement in getting back on drugs. The streets of Hot Springs are like rivers, with nice, attractive kids floating along happily, but the banks are lined with crocodiles wearing toothy grins—pushers, pimps, bootleggers, madams. I don't like to hear someone called a rat or any other animal names. Animals, on the whole, are cleaner, less brutal, and kinder to their young than many humans.

It hurt pretty bad. You always get a special concern for one of these broken birds, and I wanted to see Faye make it. But I couldn't talk about it.

"Win a few—lose a few," I shrugged.

Terry knew me pretty good, so he didn't give me a Bible verse, or anything you could see—but I knew he felt as bad as I did.

"Bring her back, Ben," he said.

"Yeah."

I didn't hear much of the service, and when we left to go to the Taco joint I automatically started looking at every girl we passed that might be Faye. I called in and got the word out: no arrest, but let me know if you find her.

The Taco Mexito had bad breath, but I braved

it and soon Elvis was working his way through a burrito. I fought an enchilada, but it won and I left half of it on the plate. I hope they gave it a decent burial. The other half lay in my stomach like a dead weight.

"Boy, that was good, Ben!" Elvis said enthusiastically. When you're six you can live like that I guess. When I was a kid I could eat coconut shells. "Where we going now?"

"My house." I paid for the burnt offering, and we went home. Elvis followed me inside, then ran to the window and looked out. "Boy, it's like being on a ship!" he cried. "Look at all the boats!"

"You like boats?"

"Sure I do,—but—I ain't never been in one."

"We'll go out for a ride. Might even catch a fish." Sonny had brought the boat back and docked it. I made Elvis lie down for an hour, then we went out on the lake for most of the afternoon.

He loved it! I let him sit on my lap and steer the bass boat, and he was good at it. Then when it got cooler I took him to a little point where I'd located a bream bed that was ripe.

I go out early in the spring and snorkel 'til I find the beds then mark them on a map. When the fish come in to spawn it's a sight to snorkel along and see them. The beds are usually in groups of about twenty. They're just donut-shaped holes in the sand about a foot across and six feet down. The females lay the eggs, then the big males hover over to keep small fish from eating them. They can't leave the nest, so if any kind of food comes close to it they are so hungry they tear at it like piranha.

I took out a lightweight Daiwa rod with a

Shakespeare reel, put a cricket hook on, added two split shot and a cork, then I baited it with a live cricket, talking to Elvis all the time.

"See, you take a cricket—hold him like this, and slide the point of the hook inside this part that looks like a collar—see? And then down into the body."

"Don't it hurt the cricket?"

"No. They're like fish. Cold-blooded." I hadn't the foggiest idea if that were true or not.

"Now, you hold it like this—no, put your fingers here. Now, we swing it back, then forward, now let go with your thumb."

He made an awful cast that went about five feet, but we were over the bed, so I knew some big daddy would like it. "When you see the cork go down, give 'er a pull."

The cork went under with a *plop* and Elvis yelled and yanked. He would have lost a bass or a crappie, but it's easy to catch bream, so he hauled and hollered and finally he landed a nice one—a red-ear that would go nearly a pound.

"Look at him, Ben!" Elvis kept saying. I looked at the boy with the sun in his hair and the thrill of pleasure in his eyes. It was one of those moments you make a picture of, and you keep it safe in some secret room you have along with a few other pictures of things you love. Then, when the bad times come, you go to the room and you get the pictures out. You hang them up in your secret little gallery and you look at them, one at a time.

I knew that if I lived to be an old, old man stuck in a nursing home without a soul to care if I lived or died—even then I could go to my gallery, pull out a picture of Elvis, standing in the sun, holding up a red-ear and his eyes flashing like he had a fire inside.

He caught twenty-seven fish that afternoon—that's not very many. I've caught as many as 150 in two hours; just pull them in 'til your arms get tired. Funny thing is, I never get tired of it; it's as much fun for me to catch the fiftieth fish as it is the first one.

But he was tired when we got back. I put him to bed and he zonked out. I had almost all the fish cleaned when the phone rang.

"Ben, it's Gina."

"Oh, you're back early. Look, Elvis is asleep. I'm going to cook some fish. You want to come here and eat—or you want me to bring him home?"

"Oh, I'll pick him up. But don't go to any trouble cooking for me."

I told her how to get to my place, and by the time I had the grease hot she knocked at the door.

"It's open!" I called out. She came in looking for Elvis and saw him asleep. "Yep. I've still got him."

She smiled and came over to the stove. "Can I help?" She smelled good—not perfume. *She* smelled good. If you could bottle that you could get rich. Girl smell.

"Set the table if you want." She began putting out my assortment of silverware, and I asked, "How was George?"

She stopped and looked down at the table, then at me. Her eyes were tired, dark smudges underneath and her mouth was vulnerable. "He's very bad. I think he's going to die." She put her hand to her mouth as she realized what she had said. "That's funny, isn't it. He may die before they kill him."

"Stop that!" I said. I picked up a whole bream and tossed it in the skillet. It sizzled at me and spit on my hand, but I ignored it and threw another bream in my other skillet. You have to have *hot* grease to cook fish right, so I always ran two skillets.

"Do your crying on your own time," I said roughly.

It was no time for tenderness. She stared at me and got angry instead of hysterical, which was my master plan.

"He's going to *die!* Don't you care?"

"That's show biz."

Her face flamed and I could see the sparks fly from her eyes. "Why you son of a—"

"Careful—there are children present." I nodded toward Elvis and she forced herself to be calm. "Gina, we don't have time to cry for George, we only have time to try to get him off. Now, get the tartar sauce from the fridge."

She looked at me for a long time, her back straight as a flagpole; then she relaxed, smiled kind of funny, and put her hand on my shoulder. "You're a fraud, Delaney," she murmured, and finished setting the table.

We woke Elvis up and he was hungry again, but he showed Gina every fish, telling her the epic tale of how he landed it.

We ate fish like crazy. Eating bream is an art. Any fool can eat a filet of bass—but what does he have? A piece of fishy-smelling fish. Now, you take bream, fried whole after being dipped in corn-meal; they're not fish, they're manna. I gave Gina and Elvis a lesson in how to eat these delicious creatures.

I gave one of my famous brief blessings: "Lord, thank you for making these fish, and thank you for letting Elvis catch them. Amen."

"You don't waste time on grace, do you, Delaney?" Gina said, "That one whizzed by so fast I almost missed it."

"I was sincere. Now, first you pick up a fish—so. Then you grab this top fin and slowly pull it out—so. Then you place your teeth against the topside of this little goody, so! Then you eat!"

The delicious white chunks fell off into your mouth with not a bone, and after a little practice, Gina and Elvis were working through the bream violently.

"That's so good!" Gina said. "Better than at the catfish place."

"Bream are better eating," I said. "Well, Elvis, you want to finish off the rest?"

"No, I'm too full." He staggered back to the bed and lay there watching TV while Gina and I cleaned up.

"Worse part of fishing—cleaning up."

"You ought to get a maid."

"On a cop's pay?"

"What is a cop's pay?"

"Rookies start at $11,500," I said.

"That's not too much."

"No, but think of the fringe benefits. We get to carry guns, and get shot at and everything!"

She didn't look at me when she said, "Not much

of a life for a woman—being a policeman's wife."
I didn't answer, and she looked up quickly.
"What's wrong?"

I laughed shortly and said, "You touched a
nerve, I guess. It's not much of a life."

We worked on the dishes in silence, then she
said, "I've got a big mouth, Delaney."

"No, it's—OK. Matter of fact, I'd kind of like to
tell you about it—about my family. I've never
been able to talk about it much.

"I never had a family. Grew up in an orphanage,
and maybe that's why I married so young. Ann
was only eighteen. I was twenty. I'd been to Nam,
but when I saw her that was all I wanted. We got
married and a year later Scott came along. He was
six years old, same as Elvis. I was on narcotics
then. Busted more than my share, I guess, but one
of them took it personal. I sent him up for dealing,
but he busted out."

I was listening to myself, and it was like someone else was telling it, except that I could feel my
lips move.

"It was one Saturday morning and I was taking
Ann and Scott to Little Rock to see her folks. We
came out of the house. They were almost to the
car. There was a shot. Then the air was thick with
bullets. The punk had got a semi-automatic.

"I saw Ann go down," I said thickly. "I ran
toward her, and then . . . Scott." I heard a sound
and looked down to see that the glass I'd been
holding was shattered. My palm was cut and
bright red drops began to fall.

"Ben!" Gina said, "Don't say any more!" Her
eyes were full, but she dashed the tears away and

said, "You've cut yourself. Do you have any iodine?"

"Sure." We did the first-aid bit, and her fingers
trembled more than mine as she put the iodine on.

She was holding my hand and I was still in some
sort of shock. I'd *never* said anything about my
family—not even to Sonny or Terry. But now I
felt—cleaned out—somehow. And for the first
time I could think about them without anger. I
looked into Gina's eyes and somehow she was like
Ann.

Maybe I pulled her close, or maybe we both
needed the security of that embrace. She was soft,
vulnerable, open, and she shivered at my touch,
lifted her head, and leaned against me. She was
breathing very steadily, audibly, deeply, and her
eyes were heavy—almost closed when I pulled
her close and kissed her.

She kissed me back, putting her hands behind
my head and we clung to each other as if there
were nothing else to hold to in the whole world.

It was just a kiss. Not of the heavy-breathing-
approaches-to-the-bed routine. We just sort of
stood there, holding on to each other, for I don't
know how long.

Then, I stepped back and said, "Well . . . sorry
about that. Didn't mean to cry all over you."

Gina smiled. "It's—it's OK, Delaney." She
seemed very calm, which I was not. "I guess I
better take Elvis home. I have to work tomorrow."

It brought me back to planet earth. It was hard
to tie this girl with Larry Proctor and the White
Orchid—but I managed.

"Right!" I said in a hard-edged tone. "The show must go on."

"What do you want from me?" she demanded. "I've got to make a living."

"Rots of ruck," I said. "I'll see you around."

She snatched the startled Elvis up, dragging him off before he could figure out what was happening. I heard the Camaro burn rubber all the way to the highway.

It was the best of times. It was the worst of times.

7

The Hot Springs Police Department is fairly well concealed. It's tucked neatly into a gully on Convention Boulevard behind a gaudy building with orange signs proudly proclaiming, "BAIL BONDSMAN."

The sloping ground is paved with native stone so there is no grass to cut. Several architects designed the building, but it was obvious they never so much as had coffee together. One of them designed the roof which is a shabby imitation of early Victorian. The main floor is modern and the basement is a rather sinister gothic—something out of Edgar Allan Poe's lesser stories.

As I went inside on Monday morning I nodded to Jabloski who bellowed: "GOOD MORNING, BEN," in his epic voice. I tried a variation and instead of screaming at him, I moved my lips silently forming the words, *Hi, Jabloski. It's a nice day, isn't it?* He apparently reads lips, because he instantly boomed, "SURE IS."

I went to my office, passing a state trooper and County Sheriff Les Majors. I had no idea what they were doing at the station. Usually the city, county, and state law enforcement units keep one another at arm's length. Actually the criminals are much closer; as Sonny put it once, "Aside from splits right down the middle based on minor issues like race, religion, politics, and personality, we function like a finely tuned watch."

Lee Parsons was the only one in the squad room. He is the only cop I ever saw who was truly 'elegant.' Dark, trim, smoothly handsome in the most masculine way. He makes his clothes look like they were personally made by Bill Blass. He gets his hair styled every week, and his lashes look fake, they are so long and thick. But they are not fake; they are real. And Parsons is real. He's a tough cop who speaks softly and calls his shots.

"Hi, Ben," he said lazily. "Jack wants to see you. I think he's mad about something. You been a bad boy?"

"I am innocent. My strength is the strength of ten—because my heart is pure."

"Well, your heart may be OK but watch your rear—'cause that's what Jack's going for."

Ameche was writing furiously when I went into his office. His eyes were red with weariness, but his voice was good. "Ben, you been mooning around for a week, now get with the program!"

"Yes, sir."

"Here!" He shoved a sheaf of papers into my hands. "There's about two weeks' work in that stuff. Now get off your can and act like a cop!"

"Yes, sir. I'll see to it."

Ameche glared at me red-eyed. "What's this humility act?" he demanded. "I know you, Delaney. You're up to something. I've got a feeling. Am I right?"

I tried to look pure in heart. "If you say you've got such a feeling, Captain, then I guess you probably got it."

He burst into laughter and came around his desk to punch me in a friendly way that would have decked Marciano. "Get out of here, you crazy ape. Try to imitate a detective for a few weeks. Marie says come see her—and bring that good-lookin' wop again. She likes her!"

I poled out and spent the rest of my shift fighting for truth, democracy, and the American way.

I lost.

When my shift was over I drove the Green Hornet to the end of the county road to Vito Lamotta's kingdom. There was a private road with a sign that would be hard to miss.

PRIVATE PROPERTY
No Trespassing. No Hunting. No Camping.
No visitors of any kind.
VIOLATORS
will be subject to immediate
Citizen's Arrest and Prosecution.

It made me feel warm and welcome.

I drove down the road feeling an itch between my shoulder-blades, but I pulled up in front of Vito's place without incident.

People with unlimited money have a problem when they build their homes: Someone always builds something bigger and more spectacular than the other barons—a new Taj Mahal.

Vito Lamotta chose to go the other way. His house didn't look like the Hilton. It was native stone and there was a deceptive quality to it. It was bigger inside than it was outside—or so I guessed. There was a gentle curve to the house that allowed it to nestle close to the shoreline. The deck was not gaudy; it concealed its massive square footage by clever design and angles that broke up the area into smaller sections.

I decided to make a frontal attack instead of crawling through a basement window. The Green Hornet looked antediluvian when I put it between a Porsche and a Volvo, but I thought smugly, *I'd show you birds on a straight track.*

I rang the bell and a maid with little bitty, close-set eyes let me in. The foyer was like the United Nations Building. It strained my eyes to see the far end of it. She asked my name and I told her I was a policeman and that I needed to see Mr. Lamotta. I waited while she went on a quest for the Mighty One.

Some teenagers tumbled in dressed in tennis togs. They were sweaty and falling down laughing over something. They smelled like money, and when they looked at me they shrugged as if to say, *Someone has to do it.*

They dissolved into the castle and pretty soon the maid came back and said, "You can see Mr. Lamotta now."

I followed her down a hall and passed into the inner sanctum where Don Vito himself got up from his rosewood desk to meet me.

"Ah. Sergeant Delaney, is it?" He was a model for an aging Cosa Nostra. Olive skin, unlined face with black eyes that probed like searchlights. Silver hair and the whole bit.

"What's the problem?" he asked.

"Were you in a big stakes poker game at the Arlington a year ago?"

Lamotta's composure broke—something that happened very rarely I guessed. The amenable smile disappeared and I saw the carnivore that lay beneath the smooth surface.

"I thought this was about—" he paused abruptly and said, "You've made a *bad* mistake, Sergeant." His eyes narrowed as he waved his well-manicured hand around. "This is my *home*," he whispered. "If you have official business, call my lawyer." He was finished with the peon and rose.

"Yeah, but I'd like to know *now*. Vito, were you really in a game at that time?"

He paused, then I saw his hand go under the rosewood desk. Almost at once the door opened and a very large man entered. He wore clothes, of course, but it was very much as if a gorilla had been carefully dressed for a role in a movie.

His body was thick, and his arms dangled lower than was necessary. A rather small head rested on a neck so thick that it was impossible to say where shoulders ended and neck began. For all his massive bulk, though, he moved easily enough, and I assumed he had done his time in the ring.

"Mr.—Delaney?" Lamotta pretended to have trouble remembering my name. "He's leaving, Leroy. Show him out."

The gorilla clamped his hand on my upper arm

and began propelling me toward the door. I shook him off and said, "I don't need any help, Leroy."

"Take him out, Leroy." Lamotta snapped. He settled back and lit a cigar. The whole distasteful affair was over for the Don.

Leroy moved forward, his brow furrowed with the effort of thought. He took my arm again, and I picked out a spot where his neck joined his shoulders. When I located it, I planted both feet, swung from the hips, and tried to drive my fist through the spot.

Leroy was driven across the room, and smashed into the wall with a crash that tilted an original Renoir worth at least ten big ones at a crazy angle. It looked better that way.

"Leroy!" Lamotta shouted. "Take him *out!*"

"Yessir!" Leroy said. He got up and this time he came at me professionally, left out in a straight line, right cocked and ready for distribution.

You can't beat a professional. They know too much and they have too much speed and power. An amateur is just a lost cause. Leroy would eat my lunch if I tried to go with the Marquis of Queensbury.

Fortunately a very sour D.I. had given me full instructions on how to handle such problems. To quote Master Sergeant Carl T. Hillis, "Hurt him bad, and he'll lose his initiative."

Leroy should have won, but when he advanced in perfect form, I 'hurt him bad' in a most unprofessional way. Roy Rogers would never have done a thing like that. He fell to the floor assuming a fetal position and keening in a very high-pitched voice.

I turned to Lamotta who had turned to stone. Taking him firmly by the arm I said, "Vito, let's talk about the meaning of life."

I pushed him back until he sat down in a mauve Naugahyde desk chair. "This is not official business, wop. I am pursuing a private hobby."

"You—you will—" The Don was getting short of breath and his face was a distressing putty color.

"Just tell me the name of the big man who was in your game at the Arlington, and I'll fade away, OK?"

Vito Lamotta was having problems. His face grew almost purple, and he fumbled at the desk drawer with impotent fingers. "In—the—drawer," he mumbled. "Medicine."

I pulled the drawer open and pulled out a little bottle of prescription pills. Nitroglycerine. "For your heart?" I asked. He nodded violently and I shook out a couple of round pills and poured him a glass of water from the carafe on his desk. "That'll be interesting to the public," I said as he gulped them down. "Most people would swear you don't have a heart."

Slowly his color grew better, and he said, "I don't—know—what you want. I was never—in such a game."

I got up, and stretched. "Yeah. You were there, wop. I'll be back to ask a few more questions—if you don't remember."

Leroy was still puling on the floor. "Get yourself some new muscle. This one won't be any good. Rest in peace Vito—real soon!"

I left the room and the maid held the door wide for me to leave. I half expected some sort of retribution, but I guess Don Vito was too shocked to react for at least an hour. And Leroy was ruined.

It was dark when I got back to town, but I still had to see the manager of that 7-Eleven where Helen Taylor had been wasted.

I filled the Green Hornet with gas and went inside. The man behind the counter was not pure black, but he was close. I took him in while he made change, and then I flashed my I.D. and said, "I'm Delaney. Want to ask you a few questions."

He took one look at my white face. The door shut—right then.

"I done told all I know to the man," he said.

"You're George Powell, right?" I said. "I want to ask—"

"*You* want to ask!" he exploded. "*You* want me to drop everything and chat with you 'bout *your* business!" Powell's voice rose, "Well, *I* got business, too, Detective Delaney! I got to take this crummy store and make it profitable! You get that—Detective Dee-laney? Profitable!" His eyes were bulging out and the big veins were throbbing.

"Take it easy, George," I soothed him. "You don't have to—"

"I don't have to do *nothing!*" he said. He made an attempt to calm himself and said, "Look, I told the department all I know."

It was a closed door. I slid out and let him simmer. Black is black, and white is white. So Sonny would have to handle this one.

It was about six when I cruised down Central to the Vine. I checked with the station: no word on Faye.

I touched down at the Vine hoping that Terry had some news. We talked for about an hour, but he didn't have anything. When I left there I just cruised the town feeling more and more like a complete idiot. Ben Delaney, disguised as mild-mannered detective, fights a never-ending battle against evil. What a crock of oatmeal!

I had been seeing myself as some kind of knight errant fighting for lost causes, a Sir Galahad in a J.C. Penney's suit.

I guess I'd sort of assumed that right would prevail, that the white hats would win, that the cavalry would arrive in time to save the settlers surrounded by the screaming Comanches.

What if I'd been wrong?

All of a sudden I thought of the time I'd been initiated into carnal knowledge of how our world operates. I'd seen about a million westerns, and in most of them there was this scene where the hero in the white hat gets the drop on Jack Elam and Elam says, "If you didn't have that gun we'd see who was a *real* man!" Whereupon our hero would toss his gun aside, and proceed to thrash Elam to the bone.

Then when I was about twelve I saw a movie that had this scene in it. I think it was Bill Elliot in *Guns of the West.* The black hat had kidnapped Mary Sue or whoever, and Wild Bill got the dirty rat under his gun, and the crook said, "If you didn't have that gun we'd see who was the *real* man!"

And I probably said to my buddy, "Oh, boy! Now watch Wild Bill give it to him."

But—the world suddenly changed, because

113

Wild Bill said, "Yes, but I *do* have the gun!" and he pistol-whipped the soup out of the crook.

Well, it changed my world. If Wild Bill in his white hat couldn't be trusted, what stability did the world offer?

Finally I drove out to Jack's house. I rang the bell and Marie met me. For once she didn't do the hugging bit. Her eyes were wide and she pulled me in nervously. "Jack is wild!" she said. "You better go in and make your peace." She looked at me with speculation in her black eyes. "He's madder than I've ever seen him, Ben. I don't understand him."

"I'll talk to him, Marie." I made my way to the study and found Jack sitting at his desk. He was shifting a Colt Python back and forth and the weapon looked like a toy in his big hands. I expected him to start yelling at me like usual, but he just sat there. I took a rest in the leather chair by the gun cabinet, and after awhile he looked over at me. His face was calm, but there was a wild gleam in his eyes, and he didn't sound right.

"Ben, you are a nuisance. I've put up with your religious spasms, but you've gone overboard."

"I guess Don Vito has gotten in touch."

"Delaney, have you gone crazy?" Jack slammed the Python on the desk. "You bust into a private citizen's home, beat his chauffeur to a pulp, and raise hell in general."

"Ah, Jack I was just—"

He came out of his chair like a cobra. "I don't want any of your smart mouth, Ben. You've gone too far this time."

I didn't like to see Ameche shook up. "He's a back number, Jack," I said.

"Back number!" Jack whispered. "You dumb mick, *no* Mafia is back number! They never give up—never!" He beat his fists against the wall and said, "Ben, you're living in some kind of dream world. Get with it! Vito is scum—but scum have teeth! They can chew the world to bits!"

I got up and wandered around the room trying to figure it out. "He knows something about the Matthews case, Jack," I said. "I thought he might help me."

"The Matthews case!" Ameche was staring at me, his mouth hanging open, his eyes wild. "The Matthews case!" He beat his head with his fist, and moaned, "Ben—Ben, we've got fifty unsolved homicides—we got cases piled up that go back five years! We got rape, arson, robbery, anything you can think of, all crying for some cop to work on it!" He looked at me with incomprehension and whispered, "And you want to chase around trying to salvage some killer who's offed a sixteen-year-old girl!"

"Jack, I'm pretty sure Matthews didn't do it. Just give me a few days——"

Jack said, "Delaney, you are receiving an official order: Get off the Matthews business!"

"I just thought we could blow some smoke down the hole and see what would come out."

Ameche shook his head and I could see that he was dead serious. "I like you Ben. Always have. You're the best man in the department. I'd say you're the man for my job when I retire in a few years. But you have to learn to let go. You're like a snapping turtle—grab on and don't let go 'til you hear thunder. Well, that's what I like. But not this time."

There was a faint tap at the door and Marie opened it and peered in. "All quiet on the western front?"

I grinned at her. "I haven't felt so bad since the principal entertained me in his office."

Marie gave me a pat and whispered loudly to Jack. "He's not a bad boy, officer. Give him a break and he'll go straight this time."

"I'll give him a break all the way back to pounding a beat if he screws up one more time."

Marie smiled and said, "Why don't you bring Gina to supper, tomorrow maybe."

"I'll ask."

"She's quality."

"Well, Marie, she's running around with Larry Proctor some and she's working in a joint."

"What were you doing when you were her age?" Jack grinned.

"Running around with evil companions in joints," I answered. "What were you doing at her age, Jack?"

"I was studying for the electric chair, I guess. Marie's right, that girl's got class. Just needs to change her ways a bit."

I got away by promising to come for supper as soon as I could; driving home I felt strange, sort of *trapped*. Or more like I was sitting helpless in a car that was racing down a road in the dark. There was something out there and a crash was coming.

I couldn't get out of the car and I couldn't see down the road.

Finally I went home and tried to sleep, but all I got out of it were some bad dreams, in living color and Dolby sound.

8

I knew Jack hadn't been kidding about working on the Matthews case, so I conducted the Matthews investigation off hours. I asked Sonny to talk to George Powell.

"He won't talk to me, Sonny. I think he's a bigot. You know how they are."

"Yeah, well I'm a brother, and if he don't talk to me, I'll open him up wider than a Baptist Bible!"

"Don't say anything to Jack. He's agin it. Matter of fact, he said not to mess with it."

"I'll use my lunch hour. Hey, I want to take the boat over to DeGray next Saturday. You wanna come?"

"Maybe. Put some air in the right tire of the trailer before you use it. Sometimes I think you only love me for my boat."

"That's a lie!" Sonny said indignantly. "I love you for lots of stuff—your rifles, your tools, your pick-up, your fifty dollars you're going to loan me. . . ." He walked off, counting 101 ways to rip me off.

I worked hard all morning, and at noon I pulled Lee Parsons out to a restaurant and bought him dinner. It came as quite a shock to him since we mostly eat at Andy's—Dutch.

When he was full as a dog tick I said, "Lee, some day you and me are going to be working together on a case. We're going to get the dirty rat trapped in an alley, and he's going to have an M-16 assault rifle and a lot of marksmanship medals from the war. It's going to be practically suicide to go after him, but one of us has to do it."

Parsons was too cultured to belch like the rest of us. He merely touched his lips with a napkin and that took care of the gas somehow. He turned his handsome face toward me and said lazily, "You're going to go into the alley, right?"

"Sure I am, partner."

"And in return for this hypothetical favor you're going to do for me, you want me to do something for you."

"It's just a trifle, Lee." I beamed. "All I want you to do is get pictures of all big time gamblers that were in town a year ago."

Lee's smoky eyes gleamed. "The Matthews thing? Didn't Jack tell you to leave it alone?"

"He didn't tell *you* to leave it alone," I pointed out. "What about it, Lee? I mean I am going to save your life!"

He smiled and said, "All right. Won't take long if you mean *big time* gamblers. Maybe twenty at the outside. Besides, I already got them."

"What!"

"You should have asked, then you could have saved yourself this lunch." He stretched like a big cat and said, "About three months ago I got a call from this writer. He's doing a book on Hot Springs and there's a big section in it on gambling. He's paying me to fill him in on the casino days and so on. But he wanted pictures—some of the clubs, like the Vapors—but what he really wanted were shots of the real high rollers. Not the two-dollar-window type. So I've got most of the big gamblers."

"Can I have them for a day?"

"I guess so. Just don't lose them; it was a lot of work. You ready?"

We went back and he gave me a large manila envelope. I took the pictures out and ran through them. "I know most of these birds."

"Names are on the back of the prints. Well, don't lose it, Ben. Thanks for the lunch."

"Do I still have to go into the alley against that maniac? I mean, it hardly seems fair since you didn't really do anything extra."

"We'll toss for it," he grinned, and we went to work.

I quit at four and went to Gina's place. Elizabeth met me at the door. "Come on in. Gina's still at work, but she'll be home by five. You wanna wait?"

"Is Elvis here?"

"Yeah, he's in his room." She smiled and said, "He ain't talked about nothin' but catching them fish since he got back. I sure do appreciate your taking him."

"Well, I enjoyed it. He's a good boy."

She said, "Sure is hard on him—being sick

most of the time, then George winding up like he did. I don't guess there's any hope, is there Mr. Delaney?"

"Call me Ben," I said. "There's hope, Elizabeth, but not very much. I want Gina to take some pictures to George. If he recognizes the man who set him up, we're in business."

"I guess I'm just wore out, Ben. Can't seem to feel anything. You want some coffee?"

"If it's made I'll have a cup." She drew one out of a Mr. Coffee and started to get Elvis. "Elizabeth, what does the doctor say about the boy? Is he getting better or not?"

She stopped and said, "Well, last time he went in—that was two weeks ago—the doctor said he seemed to be making progress. He does seem better, but it's been that way for a long time. He'll seem to get well, then he gets sick again." She shrugged and said, "I'll tell him you're here."

Elvis came in at once—with the checkerboard under his arm. "Do you want red or black?" he asked without preamble.

"Black," I said, and we played cut-throat checkers for an hour. I planned to let him beat me, but I needn't have bothered. He could pretty well beat me no matter what I planned. I watched his frowning, the tiny blue veins visible through his fair skin. He had gotten his coloring from his father, but the rest was more like his mother—large eyes, delicate ears, and wide mouth.

Between games he talked about fishing. "It was fun, Ben! I wish I'd kept one of the fish though— to show everybody."

"It'd be pretty smelly by now."

"I could have stuffed it. That's what they do, ain't it?"

"Sure, but it's not easy."

"Couldn't we use sawdust or something like that?"

"Not really. You'd have to send it off to a special place. Next time we'll save the biggest one you catch. Then we'll get it stuffed and put on a board so you can hang it on your wall."

"*Really!* When?"

"When I'm off and your mother says it's OK."

He jumped up, knocking the checkers over. Gina had just pulled in the drive. I was picking the checkers up when Gina came in. When our eyes met, it was a little strained. I was thinking of the kiss and the argument; I guessed she was too.

"I saw your car," she said. "Been here long?"

I picked up the last checker. "About an hour. Been getting my tail beat at checkers."

She smiled. "Beats me how he can do it. I've never won a single game out of about two *million*."

She was wearing her working clothes, an abbreviated silk blouse cut pretty low, a matching skirt with a slit up the front, and six-inch heels. She had on too much makeup and too much jewelry.

I guess she felt guilty or something, because she reddened when she caught my look. I said, "I've got to go talk to a woman who was a witness to the murder George is supposed to have committed. You want to come along?"

"What for?" she asked curiously.

"Well, Ameche told me to quit spending time on it, so I'm going on my own. Might be she'd feel a little safer with another woman there—and Elvis too." She looked surprised, and I said, "She's working at the I.Q. Zoo."

"Oh, I know where that is. Never been inside."

"Neither have I, but Elvis will like it."

Elvis came roaring back, his eyes bright. "Momma says I can go anytime," he yelled. "Can we go now?"

"Too late today." I ruffled his fine hair. "Maybe Saturday morning. I'm off then."

Elizabeth came in. She was smiling and I could see the beauty that worry had camouflaged. "He'll pester you to death, Ben."

"Naw, we're fishing buddies, right, Elvis? Say, Elizabeth, I'm taking Gina and Elvis to the I.Q. Zoo. You want to come along?"

"Now? I'm cooking supper. Hey, it's almost ready. You like to eat here?"

"If you got enough—?"

"There's plenty. You play one more game and it'll be on the table."

This time I beat Elvis. I watched him to see how he handled losing. People who get very good at games can get pretty hostile when they get beat. Elvis handled it fine. "I'll get you next time, Ben!" he grinned.

It was a good meal. When we sat down at the old table Gina smiled at me, "You and Elvis want to toss for who says grace?" She was apologizing for putting me on the spot at the restaurant, and I smiled to show her I understood.

"I'll do it, Ben," Elvis said firmly. He bowed his head and said the blessing. "Thank you God for the meat and the potatoes. Thank you for the bread and the salad. Thank you for the Jello that's in the refrigerator. Amen."

"Amen," I said. "That was a good blessing Elvis. Got right down to brass tacks."

"Yeah, I pray good," he said simply with no fake modesty showing. If a grownup said such a thing I'd have him put to sleep—but kids can say anything.

We had finished supper and I was helping Elizabeth clean up despite her protest while Gina and Elvis changed clothes.

"Great supper, Elizabeth. That roast was the max!"

"Ah, anybody can make pot roast," she said. For a while she stood there washing the dishes, then she said, "What's with you and Gina?"

Caught me off guard so bad I went blank. Once I got hit in the solar plexus unexpectedly, and I couldn't even breathe.

"Well—I'm trying to help George, you know?"

"Ben, I know Gina; we're real close. I'm worried about her. She ain't living right."

"She'll be OK," I muttered. "I like her a lot, Elizabeth."

"You ain't putting the moves on her, are you Ben?"

"No. I'm not much for that, Elizabeth. Never have been. I've always felt a little sorry for guys that have to have a bunch of scalps to hang on their belt. Always wonder why they're trying so hard to prove something."

Elizabeth nodded, "Yeah, I know. But she's changing pretty fast. Another year at that joint, and I don't think she'll be able to shake it off." She put the last dish away and said, "I talk to her all the time, but she don't see it's so bad. And to tell the truth, crazy as it sounds, I think she's still clean. There's guys after her, but she don't like none of 'em much."

"She can get out of it, Elizabeth."

"You interested in her, Ben? I mean like *serious?*"

I heard Elvis coming out of his room and only had time to say, "Yeah. I'm interested."

Elizabeth decided to stay home, so I loaded Gina and Elvis in the car, and we went out West Grand toward the airport. About two miles past the fork we came to a large, single-story building with a large sign outside that said I.Q. ZOO. A rabbit with a smirk on his face was jumping through the Q, and I noticed as we pulled into the lot that all six cars in the lot had out-of-state plates.

"I got a friend who's been here," Elvis said as we got out and walked toward the white stucco building. "He says they got the smartest animals in the whole *world* here." He was excited and his pale face glowed with interest. "He says they got a chicken in here that can beat anybody in the whole world at tic-tac-toe."

"We'll see about that," I said. I held the glass door open and we went into what appeared to be a large souvenir shop. There was one woman behind the cash register at the far wall and she was talking to another woman who had on purple shorts and a T-shirt that said, "What you see is what you get." I figured this was the witness, but I wanted to talk to her alone so we walked over and I said, "How much?" She looked at me through thick glasses and said in a contralto voice that sounded too large to come from such a small frame, "It's seventy-five cents per person."

"I'll take three." She gave me the tickets and we went inside the doors that led to the animals. It was a dimly lit room about 24 by 36 with plexiglass-covered cages on three walls. It was designed to let you walk along the three walls then emerge back in the gift shop.

The first cage was empty except for a small toy piano about six inches high and I could see that it was bolted to the floor.

"I don't see anything," Elvis complained.

"I think it's play for pay," I grinned at Gina. There was a slot for money in front of all the cages and I put a quarter in and waited. A door at the back flew open and a fat, white duck waddled out and stopped in front of the piano. He cocked his head and began sort of pecking and chewing on the keys, making a series of tinkling noises on the little piano. A light went on and a few grains of feed fell into a slot.

"Look at him, Ben!" Elvis cried with delight. "He's playing it. And look at him eat!"

"I like Ray Charles better," I said, but it was fun for the boy and we had to see it twice. Next tune wasn't too bad. He wasn't quite as good as Liberace, but he was practicing.

"Look here, Gina," Elvis cried and pulled us along to the next cage. "That's a raccoon, ain't it? What does he do?"

"Sign says he's a basketball player." The coon was pretty fat, so business must be pretty good in spite of the fact that there were only a few other people in the place. I dropped a quarter in the slot and a light went on in the cage. The coon ran over and picked up a little ball and with all the ease in the world dropped it into a miniature hoop on one end of the cage. Some of the food fell into a tray, and he carried it to a pan of water and began washing it.

"My, they sure are clean, aren't they?" Gina marveled.

"Actually not," I said. "They don't have any saliva glands so they have to get food wet like that." She stared at me and I shrugged. "Why can I remember stuff like that when I can't remember my own social security number?"

Within a half hour we had seen a cockatoo that roller skated, a chicken that played baseball, and a squirrel that did a trapeze act. Then we got to the chicken, the star of the show. He was an evil-looking critter, eyes filled with hate for all of us who stood on the outside. The sign said he'd never been beaten, so I put a quarter in the slot and a little board in front of me was activated and a button was in each of the nine squares of the tic-tac-toe board. I punched one of the buttons and a light went on in one of the squares. Inside the cage, a light went on and the chicken pecked at a button, causing a light in one of the squares to go on and stay in place.

"Beat him, Ben!" Elvis cried.

"I'll eat his lunch! He'll be a candidate for Colonel Sanders after I finish with him." It only took a few more punches and the chicken wiped me out.

"He beat you!" Elvis cried in disappointment.

"I can't believe a chicken could be that smart!" Gina said.

"You try it," I said, and Gina went down in defeat. Then I let Elvis try it. He had no chance. Every time we punched a button a grain of corn dropped into a hopper and the chicken ate it and waited for the next bit.

Gina and Elvis couldn't get over it. I didn't tell them that the chicken was only pecking at a button that activated a computer that was programmed to play the game. Somewhere there was a little box filled with a pound of wire and plastic that was making monkeys out of us humans.

I ran out of quarters and went to get more. The woman with the glasses wasn't talking to anyone, so I got $5.00 worth of quarters, gave them to Gina, and asked her to entertain Elvis; then I went back to the counter.

"I'm Sergeant Delaney," I said. "You're Mildred French, aren't you?" She nodded and I said quickly, "I hate to bother you while you're working but I thought it might be easier than having you come to the station."

"Is something wrong?" She leaned forward and was hugely interested. "I guess it's about the murder."

"That's right. I thought you might have thought of something new to give us."

She sighed and took off her glasses. I was taken aback. I've seen a million movies where Doris Day wears glasses for a long time and the dope can't see what she looks like, then she takes them off, and he looks like a flare went off in his mouth. He

129

stutters, "You—you're beautiful without your glasses!" I always thought that was dumb, but Mildred French who had been a mousey little librarian type with the glasses on turned into a violet-eyed siren with a sexy look that could make Rodin's Thinker stop thinking about whatever it is he thinks about.

"I've given you everything!" she said.

I showed tremendous willpower in passing up that line, and asked, "You couldn't really identify Matthews at the trial?"

"No," she breathed huskily. "He was wearing a heavy jacket and had his face covered with a ski-mask. I couldn't be sure. Didn't they ever find the gun?"

"No, it never turned up. Then you can't think of anything?"

"Not about the crime," she breathed, and leaned across the counter. "We could meet after I get off and *talk* about it, Sergeant."

I felt like David looking at Bathsheba, so it was time to git. "Well, if you think of anything, call me."

She put on her glasses, and the librarian took over. "I've told you all I know."

I had to wait until Elvis ran through all the quarters and we left. On the way back Gina asked, "Did you find out anything?"

"No. She didn't know anything."

Gina gave me a wry smile. "Foxy lady, isn't she?"

I looked at her in surprise. "Her? She's pretty drab."

"Wrong. She's got it—and I would guess you found out while you were getting change."

"Now how would you know something like that?"

"I'm a woman," she said.

"Ah, yes."

"She's a man-eater."

I thought about that. "Things are not what they seem," I said, and we went home.

We left the zoo and I said, "I need to go by the Vine. You want me to drop you off first?"

"No, that's out of the way."

"Yeah, well, it may be an hour. Every night Terry has a little Bible story for the kids. There's several new ones this week, so he asked me to sit in."

"Will it be like Sunday school?" Elvis asked.

"Well, I guess so. Can you be still for an hour?"

"Sure! I ain't no baby!"

"Don't say *ain't no*, Elvis."

"Ben said it," Elvis nodded firmly at me, and I saw my grammar was due for a complete overhaul.

The Bible study was getting underway when we got there. Terry had about fifteen kids in chairs. All of them had Bibles but I could tell a few new ones were pretty reluctant. One of them was a thick-set guy, about twenty. He looked like a picture on a post-office wall, and when he saw Gina he said audibly, "Hey, Rex, look at the chick. Mama Mia!" He got a laugh from his buddy, but Terry acted as if he hadn't heard.

"Hey, good to see you, Gina. Elvis, gimme five." We found some chairs and Terry began the lesson. As usual, his beat-up old Bible seemed to fall open at the right place automatically.

"We've been going over fundamentals for a few days, and tonight we're going to see what the Bible says. First, look at Luke 18:11." There was a ruffling of pages, whispers asking, *Where is Luke?* but Terry waited until we were all ready, then he read, "And he spake a parable unto them to this end, that men ought always to pray and not to faint."

"That's the bottom line," Terry said. "You know, I had a little dog when I was seven. We did just about everything together. We hunted together. Every time I went swimming in the creek, the little dog went in with me. We ate together. I put his bowl on the floor and when Mom wasn't looking I'd slip him a goody. . . ."

Terry was so easy. I glanced at the rough-looking guy they'd called Earl. The sneer was off his face and he listened intently. This wasn't preachy, this was a guy telling a story. Gina was caught too, and Elvis was listening so hard he almost forgot to breathe.

". . . and we slept together, too. I'd smuggle him in through the window every night and put him out in the morning. Oh, we did everything together—except one thing." He looked around the circle at his audience and said, "When I got down on my knees to pray, the little dog didn't know anything about that."

There was a hum that went around, a little laugh at the ending, then Terry said, "God made us to be with him. We studied last Friday about how man got busted in Eden, so now we're cut off. We can't see God like Adam did. We can't walk with him like Enoch did. But we *can* do one thing—what Jesus said. We can pray."

He went from place to place, verse to verse, and the air was filled with the sound of pages turning. Gina was even more helpless than I was about finding chapter and verse, so I let her look on with me, and soon Elvis was sitting very close. It was *deja vu* time. I'd done this before, or so I was convinced. Jung calls it the *collective unconscious*— that strange feeling that we've had certain experiences before. He claims the experience and memories of a million ancestors get passed on through the genes, so we're actually "remembering" what great-great-grandpappy did.

Maybe so. But I thought this was much more simple. I thought that the memory of times I'd sat with Scott on one side and Ann on the other had come rushing back. But it wasn't the bad gut-wrenching memory that had gnawed at me for months after I lost them. This was good, and I suddenly realized that every time I thought about them they were, in a way, alive again!

Terry was finishing now. He said, "Any questions?"

The heavy-set Earl looked at Terry and said, "I don't get it. All we have to do is ask God for something and we get it?"

"Well, it's not quite. . . ."

"But that ain't the way it is!" Earl shook his massive head stubbornly. "Why, I'll just ask for a million dollars! Hey, God, gimme a million bucks, please?" He looked up mockingly as if the money might flutter down from the ceiling.

Well, I won't put Earl down. I've felt about the same way lots of times. I wondered how Terry would get out of *this*. I snuck a glance and saw he was saying one of his "instant prayers," as he called them. Fire-escape praying. Once he had said, "Sometimes you have so little time you have to leave out the *Thees* and *Thous*, and just sling-shot a prayer quickly to God."

It only took a second, and nobody but me knew he'd been praying. He said, "Ben, you got your gun on you?"

Well, I expected anything but that. My neck burned as every eye in the room swiveled toward me. "Yeah, I do," I muttered.

"Take it out, will you?"

Slowly I took the Special out. One guy in the front ducked as if I were going to use it on him.

Terry turned to smile at Elvis. "You like Sergeant Delaney's gun, Elvis?"

"Boy, I'll say!"

Terry said easily, "Ask him to give it to you, Elvis. Say *please*." Elvis hesitated, and Terry urged him with a smile, "Go on, ask him."

Elvis turned to me and said, "Will you give me your gun, please, Sergeant Delaney?"

"Well—actually, Elvis—you see—" I stuttered around until Terry laughed out loud.

"Sergeant Delaney may beat around the bush,

but I can tell you his answer. It's *no—not now.* And why doesn't he give Elvis the gun, Earl?"

" 'Cause the kid might kill himself or somebody else."

"And don't you think a million dollars is dangerous, Earl?"

Oh, wow! He sunk it to him good! I felt like I did when I set the hook in a ten-pound bass and *knew* he couldn't get off. Earl was trapped, and even his buddies told him off.

"That's right, Earl baby! Couldn't hurt *you* with no million. You'd go like wild, man!"

Finally Earl grinned and looked at Terry with a new respect. "You nailed me good, Terry. I'll getcha for that!" It was in fun, and I could see Terry had them where he wanted them. He always did.

A fifteen-year-old girl raised her hand, then almost changed her mind. "Terry, can I ask you something—personal?"

"Sure, Yvonne."

"Well, why don't you pray for—for God to make your legs work?"

Most of us were embarrassed. Prayer for general things is one matter; praying for a specific thing is something else.

Terry said, "That's a good question. Very honest. And I'm going to answer it. I have prayed for my legs to be healed. And God said, '*No—not yet.*'

"Let me give you my favorite verse in the whole Bible. It's Romans 8:28. 'All things work together for good to them that love God.'

"I live on that," he said quietly. "*All things work for good* . . . doesn't say it will be fun, or easy. It does say that Jesus Christ hands us everything. So

137

when something happens—I've had to learn to say, 'This, too, is from him.' So even if it hurts, it's for good."

I thought, *Ann and Scott*. This was from him, and I knew I'd better believe it.

Terry said, "Let's stop here, and we can talk more tomorrow. Here's a list of verses on prayer. Take one and do your homework. Just a short prayer: 'Lord, you are good. Everything you do is for our good, so let us all learn to trust you for everything in life as Jesus did. Amen.' "

The meeting broke up, and I heard Gina ask Terry shyly, "Can I have one of those lists?"

"Sure, and I've got some Bibles in the office. Can you use one?"

Gina nodded.

"Joey, will you get one of those Bibles on my desk—a new one—and bring it here?" He turned to me and said, "Ben, Earl's got something you ought to hear. Hey, Earl, can you come over here?"

"Tell Ben what you told me. Will you Earl?"

"Well, I just heard some of the guys here talking about this chick, the one that split?"

"Faye?" I asked.

"That's the name. Well, I been holed up with a couple of dudes in the Velda Rose, we was gonna—." He suddenly grinned, and said, "I guess you being the fuzz I better not tell you exactly what we was gonna do."

"Wise choice."

"Yeah, well anyway we got all spaced out and somebody brought me here. That was day before yesterday. Thing is there was this chick in the room next to ours, 406, cute as a bug. She was really wired and she had this big boyfriend who looked like bad news. So I told Terry."

"I showed him Faye's picture, Ben. It's her all right," Terry said.

"Thanks, Earl. You need a favor, call on me."

"Will you give me your gun, please?" he grinned, then went back to help with the chairs.

"I think he's a live one," I told Terry. "Reminds me of me a little."

"Are you going to get Faye?" Gina asked.

"Can't just go get her, Gina," Terry said regretfully. "She's old enough to do what she wants."

"But you're going to do something, aren't you?"

"Ben, will you talk to her? She really likes you."

"Sure, but she'll have to make her own decision. I'll call you after I see her."

I collected Gina and Elvis and drove them home. Gina said when we stopped, "Are you going to go talk to Faye tonight?"

"Yeah, I am. I've got the feeling time is important."

"I'm coming with you." She wasn't asking my permission, so I shrugged and we dropped Elvis off and then drove to the Velda Rose.

We went to 406 and I knocked on the door. It opened and Faye stood looking at us blankly. Her eyes were staring and she talked in that monotone dopers use a lot. "What do you want, Delaney?"

"We just dropped by to see you, Faye. You remember Gina?"

If I'd been alone I think she'd have slammed the door, but she hesitated and I took the opportunity to barrel in dragging Gina with me. It was a nice room, but Faye was messy. Newspapers, magazines everywhere, glasses and plates with half-eaten food on the coffee table. I never knew a neat addict. "We miss you at the Vine," I said.

"I'm not going with you, Delaney, so you can just get outta here." She talked very slowly, pronouncing her words too carefully—the way drunks do to cover up. I couldn't say if she were drunk or on the hard stuff.

She sat down suddenly and glared at me. "You better get moving. I've got a boyfriend and he is jealous. Tough, too. He'd fix you, Delaney."

I saw that it was going to be tough, so I started in with all I had. "Faye, you're right back where you were before you came to the Vine—back on drugs and mixed up with some guy who'll use you and drop you when he gets bored. Remember how it was before? You were so burnt out you couldn't even feed yourself when you first came to the Vine. You made it out, but I'm not sure you can do another bit and get off."

"You bore me, Delaney, you know that? You really do bore me. Look at this room!" she waved her cigarette around largely. "Makes that crummy room at the Vine look pretty bad. My guy, he gets me anything I want—anything, you hear? I want a dress, he gets it. I want to go to the show in Little Rock, we go in his Caddy."

She paused just long enough for Gina to say very quietly, "And what do you have to do for all that, Faye?"

I guess it was like a quarterback getting blindsided. He's looking at some linebacker and dodging him, when *blam*, the free safety comes at him from the way he's not looking and tears him up.

Faye could only gasp for a minute, then she stiffened and sneered, "Well, another country heard from! You work down at the White Orchid, don't you. I can guess what *you* do, sweetheart, so don't give me no sermons."

Gina took it real good. She didn't raise her voice when she answered, "You got me there, Faye. I— I guess both of us got problems."

Blind-sided again. If Gina had hollered or screamed, Faye could go one on one, but Gina's answer didn't give her anything to aim at. "I know what I'm doing," she muttered.

The key turned in the lock and there he was— Mr. Wonderful.

"Hi, Larry," I said as nicely as I could. He gave me a look that if you could bottle it you could use it to poison cottonmouths.

"What you doing here, Pig?" He gave me his best scowl and held the door open. "You can leave now—with or without help. Your choice."

"Who writes your dialogue—Spillane?" I asked. I swear I was trying to keep it cool, but there was bad chemistry between me and Proctor. I couldn't quit picking at him and he was just itching to swing on me.

"Larry—" Gina said, and he swung around and saw her for the first time.

He took her in and then smiled with his mouth only. "Well, Gina, I guess you've got religion. I knew if you hung around with this hypocrite long enough you'd fall. Don't call me, as they say, and I sure won't call you."

"Wait a minute, Proctor," I said reasonably. "We

141

just came by to have a talk with Faye. I didn't know this was your place."

He was no dummy, and he made the right moves. He went over to Faye and if he'd tried to pull at her she might have gone with us, but he just gave her that fancy smile and said, "Well, honey, it's up to you. I know the preacher here wants you to go back to that dump on Central. I'd hate to see it, but you do what you want." He shook his head regretfully. "Sure is too bad, just when we were getting—serious. You'll miss the trip to Houston, too."

Faye was like a bird watching a snake. There's something in evil that is attractive. That's why Mitchum made it in the movies. One teenager was asked why she liked to see him and she said, *He has the most evil face I've ever seen.* Not just men either. Most of us take a second look at the women who are out-and-out wicked. It's not in the same universe with what you can feel for a woman that is beautiful and good. You figure it out.

Proctor saw her swaying and said, "Want me to help you get ready, Faye? I can drive you down if you like."

"No! I'm not going back to that dump!" Faye said. She clung to Proctor's arm and her face was flint. "It's just not for me, that's all. And don't come back, you hear?"

"Let's go, Gina," I said. "If you ever change your mind, Faye, call me."

We moved out and Proctor gave me an oily grin. "So long, preacher. Don't bother to come back—or you either, Gina."

We went to the car, got in, and started back to

the house. She didn't say a word until we got there. I got out and went up to the house with her.

"Come on in," she said. Elizabeth and Elvis were asleep but there was a note on the table: *Delaney—Call Sonny.*

I dialed and got him right off. "This is me. Did you get anything out of our boy?"

"No, and let me tell you I tried," Sonny said. "He's scared bad, Ben. He's scared of somebody worse than he's scared of me." Sonny paused and added, "I think the heat is on this thing, Ben. You better back off—and I guess you better not ask me to do any more on it either. Ameche got word I talked to Powell and he tore me up. He's mad, Ben. We better lay low."

"Yeah, you may be right. Well, I'll see you to-morrow, Sonny."

I put the phone down and looked at Gina. "I don't get it. Why is everybody so mad when I start asking questions about the murder?" But I thought I knew; when you throw a rock at a pack of dogs, the only one who'll holler is the one you hit. Somebody was getting hit, and I felt it in my bones that he was big. I saw the pictures on the table and said, "Can you take these prints to George tomorrow?"

"I guess so," she said. She took the envelope and asked, "What do I tell George?"

"Just ask if he's ever seen any of these birds. Make sure he looks at them good."

"I'll have to wait until after twelve, but I ought to be able to get back by six."

"I'll come by, OK?"

"Sure. Ben, I'm worried about Faye. I heard a

143

lot of talk about Larry, and some of it was pretty raw."

"Believe it all and you won't go far wrong. She's just a toy to him, and he'll throw her away when he's finished."

"That's where I was headed, wasn't it, Ben? And you didn't like it."

I didn't do what I wanted to and I didn't say what I wanted to. I was feeling things I hadn't felt since I had first started seeing Ann. And those little volcanoes that started erupting in you can be exciting—but they can blow you all to bits too. So I just nodded and left. Life does get a little complicated when you mess with people.

10

I had sat in an unmarked car most of the morning on a useless stakeout; as usual, watching the people parade up and down Central makes me want to jump into a tub of lanolin and soften to death. A lot of people come to Hot Springs to die. Some of these are just getting old and come to retire. The rich ones hole up in lake houses and ultimately pass on gently into that good night surrounded by doctors, nurses, and teary-eyed relatives with itching palms.

The others, those who are poor, sick, and old, you see tottering down Central almost every day. Shapeless old women carrying grocery sacks with who knows what in them. A lot of them dye their hair purple and wear short skirts with the elastic garters cutting off the circulation to their fat legs and dimestore rings turning their fingers green. The shattered old men stumble from one position to another as if they were on sentry duty. Sometimes they shave once a week, and sometimes not, and the drinkers have little to show for the thousands of dollars they've spent for booze except trembling joints, rheumy eyes, and a good run at cirrhosis of the liver.

And there are others. I had a friend once who didn't make it back from Nam, and he was fond of saying, 'Sin makes people ugly.' I found out he didn't make any moral crusade or anything like that out of it; it was just an observation. And he was right. Some of the women who drift through the clubs, the races, the hot-tub parties and all the rest, they could win a beauty contest, I guess. But there's always a hardness about them when you get close. It's like you moved in close to smell a beautiful soft rose, and you see that it's really made of barbed wire and tool steel. Most of them are fossils; they really died a long time ago and what you see is just a rag, a bone, and a hank of hair.

As I watched them flow by the car it made me think of the Black Plague of London. In those days they brought the death carts around every few days, loaded up the bodies, and threw them in a shallow hole and covered them with a few inches of dirt. Most of the derelicts that roam cities in the good ole U. S. of A.—even the rich ones— seemed to be looking for some sort of end to the business and couldn't seem to find it. O, brave new world that hath such mortals in it!

Finally I got out of the car and went into a health food place where I could keep a close watch on the office building where our suspect was supposed to be.

The tiny girl that waited on me could have been

maybe sixteen, and she was so eager to sell me some wheat germ or something she twitched her nose like a rabbit. "Have you tried some of our new aloe vera?" she twitched.

"No." I shrugged. "You got any cold juice?"

"Why of course," she hand-rubbed and said, "You can have carrot, celery, turnip——"

"How about just plain ole orange juice?"

"Oh, well, large or small?" She curled her toes disdainfully and I felt that we had passed through the crisis.

Just as I started sipping the juice I saw my relief stroll by and get into the unmarked car. It was ten 'til noon, so I gulped the stuff down and made myself saunter down the street so it would appear to no one that I was a detective doing a stakeout. When I got into the car, Janet Prescott, the only female member of the department, smiled and said, "You have to be back by one."

I liked Janet. She was really sharp and did her job as well as any man I ever saw. Her bum of a husband had deserted her and the two girls simply by going to Safeway for a loaf of bread and never coming back. When she passed the test and the government did the bit about having a percentage of women on the force, I didn't think much of it, but others did. There were the low jokes, then the innocent brushings-against, then the outright propositions. I got interested in how well she handled it. No running to the chief, no screaming fits, no calls to the local feminist group. We really became friends when Riley Pullen cornered her in a small storage cabinet and was getting really obnoxious. I started to pull him off, but she beat me to it. I saw the short blow—no more than six inches but in the right spot—and stepped back while Riley flew out backward holding his throat. He thought he was going to die of strangulation as do one and all when a hard blow takes one in the gully-gully. His face turned blue, but I comforted him by saying warmly, "Riley, you have basic lack of grace that gets more apparent with every passing year. Why don't you go to the rescue unit and suck on some oxygen for a bit? There's a good boy!"

Janet looked at me and smiled, "Thanks for coming to the rescue."

"You didn't need it. But feel free to call." We got to be that rare thing: man-and-woman friends without anything else in the offing.

I kidded her a little about being a feminist, though she really wasn't much of one. "Hey, what-tya say we go see that movie tonight, *Person of La Mancha?*"

"I've seen it," she said. "How about *Superperson*, or maybe *The Person in the Iron Mask.*"

"Maybe we better not; we'd better act like policepersons and keep an eye out for those who commit personslaughter so we can have a person-hunt."

"Get out of here Delaney," she grinned. "I have no time for male chauvinist pigs. Be back by *one!*"

While I got a really good Reuben sandwich and washed it down with sweet milk, I thought of the possibilities for finding Mister X.

There is Juan, the stoolie. Not much there.

There is George Powell. He knows something but he won't talk.

There is Mildred French. She'll talk, but she doesn't know anything.

There is Vito Lamotta. He knows something, maybe everything. But he didn't rise to the top of the criminal world by blabbing.

There is Bernie Floyd. He is probably lying, but the only way to find out would be to lean on him until he talked, and that wasn't too good either.

And the clock was running. In a few days, George would take that last walk. A voice inside demanded: What kind of cop are you, Delaney? Philip Marlowe would take about sixty-two seconds to run down Mr. X, prove that he had hired Bernie to set it up, and by the time *M.A.S.H.* comes on the governor would have issued a full pardon for George.

"You've been reading *Boy's Life* again," I told my accuser. "It's not like that. How many cases have you ever seen that came out just right? All those TV cops," I whined, "get one case at a time, and we don't. We don't have all the time in the world to sift all the evidence and make a brilliant deduction that ties it all neatly into a nice package."

"You're whining," the little voice said. "Why don't you get with the program? You're going down with your bat on your shoulder?"

I lost the little debate and in the end I called the number that Sonny had given me for Juan and made him agree to meet with me at two o'clock. He didn't like it, and I didn't see how I could get off work, and I didn't think it would do a bit of good, but it was all I could think of.

When I got back to the stakeout, the car was gone, so I knew the suspect had left and Janet was on to him. I couldn't go back to the station without getting caught up in some work, so I tippy-toed to my car and left without waving bye-bye.

I got to the gorge and about fifteen after two Juan came drifting on in, dodging from tree to tree. It made him very conspicuous and I said, "Juan, why don't you cut that out and get your rear over here." I decided to give him a little shaking up even though Sonny had told me to take it easy. These informers are necessary but they get to be prima donnas as time goes on. "How come you're late?"

"Ah, you know, Delaney, I was hangin' out in that commie bar, and these niggers and sheenies started to make a rumble. Well, I stay away from them spooks and wops as much as I can—"

He managed to blaspheme just about every racial and social group in the country except Mexicans, and I shut him off. "Never mind that. You see this? It's a hundred-dollar bill. Do you want it or not?"

His beady eyes twinkled like a welding spark. I had never seen such a case of total greed. "Yeah, man, I want it." He made a pass at it, and I pulled it back.

"Tell me about the game—the one you told Sonny about."

"I already tole him all I know, man," he protested.

"For a C-note you can maybe remember better. Start talking and I'll tell you when I got my hundred bucks' worth."

He shrugged and told the story again, just like

he'd told Sonny. Then I began to pick at it. "Which chair was Vito in?"

"He was—right in front of the window."

"Who was on his left?"

"I don't know, Delaney! I ain't ever seen him before."

"What did he look like?"

On and on it went. People remember more than they think and part of a cop's work, maybe the biggest part, is to worm it out of them. I went on with Juan and was just about to give up. I said, "You're not trying, Juan. No C-note."

"What!—wait a minute! I just remembered something!" he said, and I saw that he really had. The sight of the money had dredged it up from his subconscious. "There was this guy, and he didn't play, but he was always there. And he kept on talking to Vito and to this other guy that I didn't know, the big one." (*Mister X*, I thought.) "And I'd seen him before, maybe a couple times."

"Describe him." The kid had a good eye for detail, but it wasn't going to help much. I had to get something that I could see. But what?

Janet Prescott. If I hadn't seen her just an hour earlier I wouldn't have thought of it. Janet has one talent that got her the job. Aside from being a woman she was a gifted artist. She was, in fact, our sketchperson—the one that draws charcoal sketches from verbal descriptions given by eyewitnesses.

I tore the bill in half and gave it to Juan. His eyes bugged, and he cursed in his native tongue. "What you do that for?"

"You get the other half after you do one more little thing for me."

"What's that?"

"Come to my house and tell someone else what this guy looked like."

"No!" he said and looked around. "It's too risky, man."

I have practically unlimited faith in the power of greed. I snatched the half-bill out of his hand and said, "OK. Blow, Juan."

"But the money?"

I held up both halves of the bill, piecing it together and said, "All yours—just one little trip."

I dropped him at my place and went to find Janet. I couldn't get in the station, so I stopped at a phone booth and put a handkerchief over the receiver, then dialed the station. When Jabloski answered, I did my best German voice, "Iss Fraulein Bress-kott dere?"

Jabloski bellowed, "WHAT? OH, YEAH. I'LL PUT HER ON."

I waited and she came on, "Officer Prescott."

"Diss is Herman von Kreikenhorn. I haff blease to zee you—"

"What do you want, Delaney?" she asked in a bored voice.

"Oh, you recognized me? I better work on my accent. Listen Janet, you know that favor you owe me?"

"What favor?" she asked sharply.

"Any favor. Now listen, I want you to tell the boss that Amy is sick and you have to go to school to pick her up."

"Shove it, Delaney," she said sweetly. "I'm trying to create a career and I don't need—"

"Janet—this is important to me. I need you."

Silence, then she sighed, "All right. Where do I meet you?"

"I'm parked at the Ramada Inn. Get in my car and leave yours there." I hung up and waited.

It was only about ten minutes, and she slid in with a peculiar look in her eyes. "I don't like this, Ben. What's up?"

I moved out and headed home. "Want you to listen to a little Mexican canary, Janet. Then I need a picture."

"You could have brought him to the station."

"No. Jack told me to let this case alone."

"So you drag me into it with you."

"Yep. That's what friends are for, Janet. 'A friend loveth at all times, and a brother'—well, a sister in your case—'is born for adversity.' I've got the adversity and you were born just to help me with it."

"Take me back." Her eyes were hard and she said, "I like you Ben, but I lost too much by trusting a man. I won't do it again."

I kept on driving. "Nope. You're not going to live like that, sweetheart. You're ruling out the whole world just because of one guy. You want your girls to distrust the whole world?"

"Most of it's not worth trusting," she said. "Why should I risk everything for you?"

"Because you know if you need me—I'll be there. Ain't that the truth?"

She thought it over and said, "Yes! And it'll get

me hung someday. What's that thing you said, 'A friend loves—'"

"It's in the old book. 'A friend loveth at all times, and a brother is born for adversity.'" I drove a little faster, and looked at her with my most charming smile. "If I counted up all my friends—and I mean all, those from the army, from school, on the force, at home, all of them— you know how many I'd muster?"

"How many?"

"About four or five—and I think you made the cut, Prescott."

"That's nice, Ben. . . . I guess I get a little hard sometimes. It's just that I'm afraid for my kids."

"They're gonna be all right," I said. "I guarantee it."

We pulled into the drive and Janet stopped suddenly and said, "I don't have any paper or charcoal."

"You are dealing with a police officer who never fails to anticipate the needs of his fellowpersons." I held up the sack of things I'd gotten from the drugstore while she was on her way.

We went in and Juan was about to take off. I calmed him down, got Janet seated, and then had Juan go through his bit.

"Well, he's a big guy, maybe even a little taller than Delaney here. And he's got sort of light blond hair that's styled, you know. Kind of grows low on his forehead. And it turns up in back."

He went on and on while I fixed coffee. When he faltered, Janet asked him a question, then drew some more lines. Finally she said, "This is about the best I can do."

I took it from her and held it up to the light. It was a good sketch all right.

I guess Janet must have been looking at me, because she said, "You make him, Ben?"

"Yeah, I make him all right." I put the picture in a folder and said, "Juan, where you want to be dropped? Oh, here's the bill."

"All *right!* Just keep me out of it, OK? Take me to the fountain."

We got in and I dropped Juan, then asked Janet, "You want to go to the station?"

"Too late. Take me to the car. I have to pick the kids up. And I have to convince Amy that she was sick today—in case somebody asks."

I waited 'til we got to her car and she was getting out. I took her arm and squeezed it. "Hey, I owe you one, all right?"

"Sure, Ben. I'll ask."

A good guy, Prescott. I remembered suddenly a couple of lines from a poet named John Wink:

There are pockets of loveliness
Splashed on the dark, stained earth.

I wanted Janet to come out all right, so many were coming out wrong. I wanted her girls to grow up to be tall, lovely, chaste women adorned with virtue. I wanted that family to overcome all the hidden traps, the baited lures, the hidden razor blades in the candy and the needles in the apples. I wanted to read one day that good things had happened to them. I wanted them to live happily ever after.

Who says that can't happen?

I was sure that Gina would be home, and she met me at the door with eyes that were like sparklers. She said breathlessly, "He knew him, Ben! Here, this is the one George said was at the game!"

I looked on the back of the shot and read the name, "Mario Taliferro. I don't know him."

"He's sure!" Gina said. "He seemed to come to life when he saw the picture."

It wasn't a mug shot. Some photographer had made the picture as Taliferro was being arrested coming out of the Vapors. He looked well-heeled and much better off than the officers who were making the arrest.

"I better get to the station and get the word on him," I said.

"Do you think you can find him?"

"Should be able to—but we don't have much time." I didn't want to put out the light in her eyes, but I said, "Gina, I've been disappointed a lot of times. Don't—don't get hurt too much if it doesn't work out."

"I can't promise that, Ben. It's got to work out. Don't you think it's possible?"

"Sure, anything's possible—"

"About all that prayer thing that we heard last night, don't you believe any of that?"

"Gina, you have a way of making me feel rotten! Sure, I believe in prayer, but I'm just—I just don't have very much faith, I guess."

"Elvis does," she said. "When he said his prayers last night, he asked God to bring his daddy home. Now you tell me, Delaney, because I want to know—do you really believe all this God stuff, or are you just faking it?"

I thought about it a long time. I even slumped down in a chair and tried to think of some way to explain how I felt. Finally I said, "I'm not faking it, Gina. I'm just not very good at it. When I lost Ann and Scott, I nearly went crazy. I turned to the bottle, and if Jack Ameche hadn't pulled me out of it, I'd be dead, I guess. He put me to work, but it was Terry that did something else. He'd been a great athlete, but he got caught in the middle of a gang fight he was trying to stop and got paralyzed from the waist down. I was there when he had to testify against the punk who shot him—and I guess that's what got me started thinking about God. There wasn't any anger in him. I couldn't believe it, Gina! He wasn't one bit mad, and I started hanging around the Vine, and pretty soon I found out that what I'd always thought about religion was nothing very close to what Terry believed.

"Well, I kept on living, but I was mad. I hurt a lot of people, and one day Terry told me I was really mad at God for taking my wife and boy. And he was right!"

"What did you do, Ben?"

"I just flat got to the end of everything, Gina. And when I did I just called on God. I don't know much about theology, but I know that Jesus Christ is *real*—and I know prayer is real too." I took a deep breath and said, "I'll believe it, Gina, that George will come home. I—always feel a little silly when I do things like this, but it's fish or cut bait I guess."

She didn't answer and finally I asked, "Do you believe it, Gina?"

She put her hands together and said, "I haven't believed anything in so long, I don't know if I can."

Then I remembered the envelope. I took the sketch out and showed it to her without a word.

She looked at it strangely and her face burned. "Why are you doing that, Ben? To shame me?"

"No!"

"Why else would you show me a picture of Larry Proctor?"

"He was in the game, Gina, the game where George got cleaned. It means that he knows the guy who set George up—Mister X."

Gina shivered. "It's hard to believe I liked him, Ben. But he could be—"

"Sure, I know. But now we're gonna have to put foots on our prayers, as the saying goes."

Gina looked up quickly and put a hand on my arm. I guess she must have seen something wrong in my face. "What are you going to do, Ben?"

"It's only a few more days. We don't have much, just a few people who might know something. Somebody is going to have to open up. And, I guess I'm the official opener."

"You don't like it much, do you, Ben?"

"No. There's going to be some bodies around before this is over. I've felt that pretty strong. I'm going to be pretty busy for a while, but I'll call you if anything comes up."

I went down to the station and started the check on Taliferro. He had to be somewhere.

We all do.

11

I did all the things we do to locate people who usually don't want to be found. I wasn't as sure about finding Taliferro as I had let Gina think. All these tools that modern police use are pretty fancy, and they're wonderful when you're writing scripts for television detectives. Usually they aren't worth much. I have yet to see one murder case ever prosecuted successfully as a result of fingerprints. All the vast networks and computers of the FBI, the CIA, state police, and all the rest of it can't find a guy who really doesn't want to be found. Forget about Ironside's wheeling in with a steely command, "Run this through the files," and in twenty minutes one of his comical sidekicks rushes in ecstatic, waving a slip, and saying, "He's living at Bucksnort, Tennessee, under the alias of Lawrence Smellfungus disguised as a chicken-sexer."

So if Taliferro wanted to be invisible, he would be invisible. But lightning might strike, so I sent the description and told Stanfill, the sergeant on duty, to call me as soon as the word came.

I picked up a barbeque at Stubby's and wondered what to do next. The options were numbered. Finally I decided to take another crack at Bernie Floyd. I wasn't sure if I ought to scare him or bribe him, so I decided to play it by ear.

I went to the Holiday Inn and knocked on the door to Suite 9A, but it was answered by a woman about fifty with arms like Arnold Schwarznegger and dressed for a party. "Well, *hello*, big boy. Come on in and make yourself at home." She leaned forward and I had never met anyone who had breath more like Mace.

"Well, actually I just want to see Bernie."

"Bernie? No one here by that name, but I'm in the mood for a big time!" She clamped her hand on my arm and started hauling me in like she was a Warn winch. I left two heelmarks through the doorway, and broke her grip by using Basic Defense Move Number Six in the *Karate Journal*.

"Gee whiz, I'd like to stay, but I'm on duty." I tried to look sorry, but she lost interest when she found out I could break her grip. "You been here long?" She slammed the door, and I went down and asked the clerk when Bernie had left. He hadn't been gone long, the boy said, so I left and drove to the joint where he mostly did his two-bit gambling.

The Red Pony was just about as seedy as most of the other joints in Hot Springs. A lot of blue neon, windows all painted over, local cars nuzzling the white square cubicle just on the edge of the business district. Inside were the usual zombies propped up by a long bar, and people floating around like fish in an aquarium darting here and there to shout intimacies over the din of about a hundred others determined to shout their own. Over all this was the raunchy beat produced by several hirsute young men wired for sound. There was the electric guitar, bass, drums, all of them making whining noises as if they were in great pain, faces twisted into an expression that you ordinarily associate with food poisoning.

I made my way through the room, which was not hard for I had a good blocker in front of me. One of the bouncers, a black about five feet tall and five feet wide, was parting the sea like an iceberg. I didn't see Bernie, and I was on my way out when I saw Mario Fuceri leaning against the wall. He was in the shadows glaring at me, and I went right at him. He was a rotten punk, but he was a pal of Bernie's. We had been sick of one another the first time we met—perhaps because I was busting him for dealing dope on the playground of a grade school.

"Hi, Fuceri," I said, and nodded to the small dark girl who clung to him like a barnacle. "Still shooting up?"

The girl looked at me with an open mouth, then pulled away from the hood. He was pretty rough with the local talent, and I saw that she expected to see him work me over.

"I don't wanna talk to you, Delaney," he said thickly. He tried to move on, pulling the girl with him, but I nabbed him by the lapel and pulled him back.

"I need to talk to you, Mario."

He jerked away and said, "We ain't got nothing to talk about, cop."

I stepped in close before he could stop me and grabbed a hunk of side meat. I have these big hands, and when I squeeze it is sort of ultimate. He tired to jerk away and I showered down on him; he cried out and reached for my hand, but I just sort of lifted him up against the wall. He'd have a blue copy of my hand for a few days, but it improved our relationship. "You changed mouthwash, Mario. I liked the other one better."

"You—you're tearing me—to pieces—!" he gasped.

I eased off and let him down but kept my grip ready to encourage him if he got sullen. "Where's Bernie Floyd?"

"I don't—OW!—I ain't seen him—honest!"

"All right, where's he live?"

I encouraged him and he said quickly, "Over on Pine Street. I think it's 316." I let him go, and the look he gave me would melt lead. The little audience which had collected during our interview found something else to look at, and I left with no new fans made at the Red Pony.

It wasn't hard to find the address, but it was a milk run. It was on one of those hillside streets with houses leaping up over one another, and years ago it had been a pretty classy neighborhood. Time had gnawed away at it, and now the steps were crumbling, the paint was flaking, and the porches were sagging. Number 316 was a stucco job, a small place with a single door and two windows in front. It had a tile roof that had been top of the line back in the twenties, but many of the tiles had cracked and several were missing.

I looked around but the whole street was dark. No sense missing a golden opportunity like that, so I stepped inside. The lock was one of those that use the old round keys for sale at every variety store. I took a chance and turned the lights on. It was a dump, but I hadn't expected anything else. I had some time on my hands, so I set out to search the place. "How doth the busy little bee improve each shining hour," as the saying goes.

You can't hide anything from a man who knows how to look. I didn't have time or help to do a complete search, but I did pretty well, and two hours later when I left, I was convinced that Bernie had left nothing that I could use. He was either clean or smart enough to stash anything interesting somewhere else. I don't even know what I had expected to find. Maybe a gun that would be traced to the hold-up, maybe some letters that mentioned that he'd done the job, or even an address where he could be. I had the feeling he was flown. And I guessed that I had scared him off his nest.

It was after midnight when I pulled up in front of the house. I locked the car and went in. I've always thought that old hokum about instinct was overdone. The time I got put down in Nam I was feeling better than I had for months. Time and time again I had this "feeling" that I was about to get it, and I never did. Then one beautiful spring day when I had just had a great meal, a sniper got me in the thigh from about a mile away.

And that's what happened when I stepped inside. It was dark. I shut the door and reached for the plate, but they saved me the trouble. The lights went on and at the same time two guys who were standing on each side of the door clamped down on me and put both my arms in a come-along. A guy who can do it right can make the world's champion horseshoe bender move in any direction. When you've got both hands locked in, it's sad.

"Well, well, Officer Delaney. We thought you'd never get here."

Larry Proctor was sitting in *my* chair, and I guessed he'd been eating from *my* bowl and would soon be sleeping in *my* bed. He got up and walked over to where the gorillas were holding me almost off the floor and slapped me across the face just for starters. "You don't look happy, Ben. Do you think he looks happy, you guys?"

The one on my right I knew to be an ex-pug named Tony something. He gave my arm another hitch and said through his busted nose, "Ah, Larry, he looks real happy to me."

The other one just snarled and gave me a twist that brought me almost off my feet. I glanced at him and gasped, "Has this one had his distemper shots, Larry?"

Proctor laughed, and slapped me another one just for fun. "You kill me, Delaney, you know that." Then he said, "Hey, put the cop in the chair—he's probably tired from arresting crooks all day."

They walked me over to a straight-backed kitchen chair, and wheeled me around without losing their grips. I hit the chair, but they held my arms straight out in the come-along. Proctor reached inside my coat and lifted my gun.

He stood over me a minute; I thought he was going to give it to me there, but he stuck it in his belt and said, "Listen good, cop, because I'm not going to say this but once. You been making a nuisance out of yourself, poking your nose in where you got no business."

"Larry, do you have these guys hired by the hour?" I asked.

"What?"

"Because it's going to cost you a bundle to pay them for holding me the rest of my life. Sooner or later they're going to have to go to the potty—if you got them housebroken—and then I'd be—" The guy on the left had no more expression on his pan than an old biology textbook, but he must have had his feelings hurt because he hoisted my arm up so high it nearly went out of the socket.

"Let him down, Mac," Proctor said. He looked at me with a funny look and said, "If I had my way I'd feed you to the fish. But I'm gonna offer you an out. The word is you don't take no kickbacks. But you better take this one." He pulled a package out of his inside pocket and peeled back the newspaper it was wrapped in. There was lots of green inside. "Ten thousand, Delaney. You get that as a bonus. All you got to do is gimme your word you'll sit tight on the Matthews killing until the 20th—then you can do what you please."

"I think better with my arms hanging down," I said.

"You think I care what you want!" he snapped. "You hang there and make up your mind—and I hope you say *no!*"

"What makes you think I won't take the money and cross you up?"

Larry opened his mouth to answer, then changed his mind. "I ain't gonna argue with you. Is it a deal or not?"

My mind went into high gear; thoughts blurred as they flew thick. Something was wrong with all of this. It proved that there was something to George's story, because someone was jumpy enough to put the heat on me. But it was the wrong kind of pressure. If it was Don Vito behind it, he would have me killed out of hand, not all this business with the bribe. If Proctor had his way he'd rub me out as neatly as possible. It didn't make any sense at all.

"Time's up, Delaney," Larry grinned. "You want the dough? Or you want something else?"

He was standing right over me and I could see the butt of the Special right in his belt. If I had just one hand free I could have snatched it out, but I didn't. What I needed was some new variation of the old "Your shoelace is untied!" routine. There wasn't any and I never believed anyone had ever in the history of the world fallen for that anyway. There was only one way and I took it. It involved something that a couple of years ago would have been automatic. All I had to do was say, "I'll take the money." But I knew that I wasn't going to stop, no matter what Proctor and his goons did.

It was situational ethics that nudged at me; that excellent philosophy which provides a valid excuse for doing what you want to do. Basically it says that there's nothing right or wrong—it all depends on the situation.

Well, the situation seemed to be that if I didn't tell a lie I was going to get wasted, George was going to be fried, and Elvis' prayer would be short-circuited. It was one of those areas of faith that some people might have handled, but at the moment I just couldn't adjust. "I'll take the money, Larry," I said.

He looked disappointed, then he shrugged and said, "I thought for sure you was gonna be a hero, Delaney. But I knew all the time you was a phony. OK, let him go."

The baboons dropped my hands and I had to flex my fingers and arms to get the blood stirring. "Hate to disappoint you, Proctor, but I guess I'm no hero."

He sneered and started to turn. I took my chance, and it was a pretty short one. Mac and Tony were right beside me, and they weren't the brightest stars in the firmament, but they were probably fairly fast. They were packing heat, I figured, and Proctor probably was too. But it was the only game in town. I knew that no matter how many times Clint Eastwood takes on five guys and beats them into mush, it wouldn't happen like that for me.

I reached out with my right hand toward the Special stuck in Proctor's belt, and I almost made it. He saw me coming and swayed back just enough so I touched the butt but never got my hand on it. I knew there was only one chance then, maybe one in a thousand, but I took it. Mac and Tony were both moving and I simply brought both arms forward, then swung them back as hard as I could, swinging for the groin. I was about the right height, sitting down like that, and I put Mac out of it with a direct hit. He let out a muffled cry and fell to one side, but I missed Tony and I had time to do no more than tighten my neck muscles when he hit me there and knocked me to the floor. I rolled over, bumping into Mac, and started yelling with all my might—not just words but really screaming.

If you ever get in a mess with someone trying to hurt you—try yelling. It's like setting off a burglar alarm, and even if there's no one to hear you, the attacker will sometimes get rattled and make a break for it.

I did fairly well until Larry leaned down and gave me a chop right in the throat with the hard edge of his palm. I kicked his feet out from under him and scrambled up making for the door, but Tony was too quick. He slammed into me from behind, driving me into the wall with a crash that shook all the pictures loose. He sledged his fist into the side of my head, and things started getting sparkly. I reached behind him, grabbed his hair, pulled his head back, then butted him in the mouth with my head. I felt some of his teeth go, I thought, but I had no time to enjoy it, because Larry was standing over me. I couldn't dodge the chop he gave me, and it put me down like a bowling pin. I could see that Mac had come around and was moving toward me; then Proctor and Tony whipsawed me, catching me on both sides of the head with club-like blows that ended it.

I was out only for a few minutes, I think, but when I came to I was back on the chair with my arms in the double come-along. I looked up at Tony and said with a thick tongue, "Well, there's nothing new under the sun." He gave me a mean twitch, and then Larry came through the door. I thought he had a gun in his hand.

"You know, cop, I'm kinda glad you did that. Now we're gonna give you a little ride."

"Is this *it?* as George Raft would say?" Then I saw that it wasn't a gun in his hand. He held up a hypodermic needle and it glinted in the light of the lamp.

"Hold him, don't let him move," Proctor said, and they twisted my arms until I nearly passed out. It was so painful that I hardly felt the prick of the needle in my bicep.

Proctor put the needle in his coat pocket and said, "You can let him go now. If he tried to run he wouldn't get to the street."

I felt them let go of my arms, and I got up. It must have been potent stuff, because I felt the heat rush up my arm, and my head was light in a few seconds. I knew that this was as close to death as I'd ever been, and I wondered how Larry would get rid of the body. I had a great sadness as I thought of Elvis and Gina and Elizabeth. I saw that the three of them were waiting for me to say something, but I didn't have anything to say.

Suddenly there was a sort of mushroom explosion in my mind, not painful, but just blossoming out. It was a warm, echoing thing that spread through my head and made Proctor's face blur into a bulbous orange mass, then fade. The room

169

was falling away beneath me, and there was the sound of a wind rushing as the mushroom continued to fill my head; then the sound began to die out, the orange mushroom began to fade, and I fell through layer after layer of soft, colorless clouds, never hitting the ground.

It was not like being knocked unconscious in a ballgame or by an explosion, both of which I have experienced. I was not unaware of the things that went on. It was more as if I knew they were happening, but it seemed that they were happening to someone else. Once I went to a dentist to have some serious work done, and the dentist gave me laughing gas—nitrous oxide. He put the little mask over my face and told me to breathe. I really didn't feel much different, and it came as a little surprise that I didn't drift off into a deep sleep, but I didn't. He began the work, and I was very much aware of every move he made. But it was so *detached*. When the drill hit the tooth it was painful. I almost said, "My gracious, that certainly does hurt!" But it was only a clinical observation, and I was only mildly concerned that it was Ben Delaney that was being hurt.

Now I felt a car beneath me, the wheels striking small bumps, and the carpet pushed into my face, but it wasn't particularly important. Someone was talking about me and saying things that had to do with my future, but I wasn't interested. Finally the car stopped, and I felt someone drag me from the back seat. My head slapped against the steel chassis but the pain was academic.

It was dark, and when we went inside I saw the

lights in the bulbs overhead and there were some people in white and they were all half carrying me along and talking as we went. I guess the dope was beginning to wear off because the words began to make sense—not a lot because they floated in and out of my mind like butterflies, but I began to pick up a little.

". . . him outta here . . . said to keep him 'til . . . he's a tricky . . . got to watch him like a . . ."

That was Proctor, then a face loomed into my vision. Somebody with big lips like sausages and eyes like bowls of chili began to breathe on me, and he was saying something—". . . take care of it . . . won't let him wake up 'til . . . bring the money . . . put him in the . . ."

I felt myself being piloted down a hall, then through a door. When someone threw me into a bed, my head slapped against the headboard and I felt the beginnings of pain. It was kind of like it woke up my brain a little because I heard Proctor talking in whole sentences.

"What about the nurses? If he gets a chance to talk to them he might convince one of them to call somebody or to turn him lose. He's gotta be kept out of it 'til next Tuesday."

Sausagelips was saying, "Cool it, Larry. I'll put Sam with him and keep the nurses out. We'll keep him coked to the gills, so when Sam sleeps, he sleeps."

I guess I moved and made some kind of noise, because Proctor said, "Hey, he's awake."

"He won't be for long." Sausagelips went out of sight and I tried to roll over, but all the signals were down, and Proctor laughed at me. Then Sausagelips was back with a needle and he gave me a shot that I never felt. . . .

I heard the door shut, and they went off down the hall. I looked at the door, but it was farther away than Central America. I tried anyway, but about all I did was lift both eyelids about one thousandth of an inch. Then the dope hit me. I fell into a deep, dark, silent well and I was making some kind of silent scream as I went down.

12

Off the coast of Belize lies the most beautiful coral reef in the world. I was there swimming lazily along in the blue-green waters clear as cellophane. The water was so warm and light that I didn't use my tanks; I just inhaled the water as I swam along far under the surface. Faint gurgling sounds drifted through the waters, and sometimes I could hear a voice and feel hands pulling at me.

One of the fish drew near, a mountain of a jewfish. He opened his maw and I could see the feathery gills and the bony track leading to his gully, white as alabaster. Then he dissolved and a gray catfish came mucking along, suctioning as he went, followed by a thin-bodied darting form that slashed at my face with his grinning mouth. A soft-bodied snail advanced through the waters and began to crawl over my face. He had rough jaws and began moving up my cheek and toward my eyes, and I began to claw at my face, twisting and flailing through the waters.

I struggled out of the depths, choking as the briny waters filled my lungs. I knew I was drowning.

But I surfaced from that deep, dark tunnel we call the unconscious, and I saw that I was in a bed in a room. There was one window with blinds pulled. The room was dark except for the twenty-gallon aquarium that had a large molly and a few darting silver fish I didn't recognize, and one lazy snail groping across the front glass. A pale green light glowed and I stared into it trying to put some of the pieces together.

My mouth was dry as the Sahara and my eyeballs crackled when I raised my lids. They kept trying to fall and I didn't have any toothpicks to prop them up with. I knew that I had been drugged to the max, and when I tried to lift my hand to wipe my eyes, nothing happened. All the wires were down, paralyzed by the dope. I felt like a big bug that some spider had pumped full of her juice and left to ripen.

It began to come back, but like a montage with no time sequence at all. I could see Larry and Sonny swimming together in one frame, then Elvis floating through the air and Elizabeth trying to catch him. Nothing made much sense, and for a long time I just lay there like a potato buried in a mound of dirt. Then I began to sort things out. I could remember that Proctor had shot me full of dope, and I knew that someone had done the same several times. How long I'd been in this room I had no idea. I did know that for some reason I should get out as soon as possible.

About the time I was getting ready to try another arm lift, I heard the door open, then the light came on. I had my eyes cracked just a slit, and I could see this big guy in a white orderly uniform come in and stop by my bedside. He was whistling "The Halls of the Mountain King" off-key and seemed to be happy in his work. He began talking to me like you talk to a dog or horse you're going to doctor up.

"OK, buddy, wake up a little. That's the way." He slipped his arm behind me and lifted me up. He was strong and that was discouraging. But he put a glass of water to my lips and said, "Can you drink a little for old Sammy? Sure you can! That's the way—easy now, don't strangle—that's the way!" I gulped for quite awhile, then he said, "OK buddy, we're going to try a pill 'stead of that big ole needle. Come on, swallow this like a good guy."

He jammed a big pill in my mouth, and I had sense enough to do just what I'd done when my mother shoved pills in my throat when I was a kid. I put it under my tongue and then swallowed the water he fed me. "Open up, now—let Sammy see if you got it—ahhh, that's a good boy. Now you lay down and drop off and I'll be back to give you another pill real soon."

He dropped me back on the bed and left. I moved my tongue around retrieving the pill, but I couldn't move my arm to take it out, so I just blew it out across the bed. The shot was wearing off, and eventually I was able to roll over. I pulled myself up by the back of the bed, and sat there weaving and swaying for a long time, then I got my feet off the bed and on the floor. I found the pill on the bed and realized I'd have to get rid of it somehow. I knew I couldn't flush the pill down the toilet, because Sammy might hear the sound. My eye lit on the aquarium; I crept toward it, holding onto the bed, then making a wild grab for the wall. Finally I got to the tank and dropped the large white pill inside. It settled on top of the multi-colored marbles that lined the floor. I thought it would melt, but it was invisible anyway.

While I waited for the next pill, I kept awake by any method I could. I counted the tile on the ceiling several times. I named all the states and put them in their place, I went through all the Marx Brothers' movies and was surprised to discover that I had practically memorized them. I quoted all the Bible verses that Terry had marked for me to learn.

Time after time I almost slipped into another coma, but finally the door opened and Happy Sam came back and did his thing. "Four hours, buddy. Another pill—well, two this time, 'cause I'm gonna catch a little shut-eye myself." He put one pill under and I stored it in the hidey-hole, then the second. "Drink a little water, buddy—now let Sammy see—." He pulled my jaw down and peered inside. "That's the way, buddy." He let me flop back and I let my head fall awkwardly to one side. He pulled it up and set it on the pillow. "See you later, buddy." He left whistling "The Dead March" from *Saul*. Maybe I can whistle a tune for you, buddy, when you come back with your little pill.

I was feeling better, but I knew that I had to use the time to get ready. The dope they'd shot into me wasn't done yet, and I kept trying to slip off into a sleep. When I got sleepy, I got up and made myself walk around the room. I wanted to open the window and get some fresh air, but it was too dangerous.

I did fine for about four hours, then I caught myself in a catatonic trance. I lurched off the bed and beat my head with my fist. What's the matter, you can't miss a night's sleep? What about Daniel in the lions' den? Think he went to sleep? Well, on the other hand he probably did, but there are others. What about Jonah, hey, what about him? I began telling myself about how Jonah probably didn't get a decent night's sleep during his whole trip. And what about Paul and Silas? Well, what *about* them? Why, you cluck, when they were locked up in that Philippian jail, did they sleep like zombies? They did not! Well, I ain't no Paul. We can't all be supersaints, can we?

Finally I talked myself out of my sleepiness. I walked the floor and did everything I could to get myself alert. The time crawled by, and I had no way of judging how much had passed.

One thing I knew: I couldn't handle Sammy without some sort of weapon. If I hadn't been doped up for so long, I would have jumped him and maybe come out on top. But I had no way of knowing how long I'd been out—maybe one day or more, and I was weak from not eating.

So what do I use? I looked under the bed for a slat, but it was one of those without slats. There was no heavy vase or anything else I could lay him out with. I thought of making a strangle noose out of the cord from the blind, but that took too much strength and agility. He had to walk up to where I was lying on the bed, and I had to get him when he bent over.

I turned the place upside down and inside out. My clothes were in the closet, but only my shoes had any weight, and not enough at that. The closet pole was lightweight aluminum, so that was no good.

I was getting pretty jumpy. It was going to be a one-time affair. I either got out the first try or not at all. No way to practice. You know how your mind gets to fluttering like a bird in a cage when things begin to close in and you don't see any way out. I'd had it happen before, and it's no fun. It got pretty bad and I was hyperventilating a little, gasping in short breaths, and then a thought came at me. I thought of a sign that Ted Bentley, a friend of mine, had on his desk: WHY PRAY WHEN YOU CAN WORRY?

Pray? This is no time for that! God gave us common sense, didn't he? I thought. Well, this was no time for common sense. It wouldn't work. So, I just laid back and said, "God, get me out of here." No Thees or Thous or fancy stained-glass language. I remember an old preacher once saying, "Prayer isn't fancy talk; prayer is backing the truck up to the loading dock and getting God to fill it up." I thought that was pretty crude, but this was no time for theology.

Well, I guess the shrinks would say that I had practiced self-hypnosis, but I got a real calm feeling. Just felt like it was all right. Nothing had really changed. Old Sammy was waiting in the wings with his junk, I was still weak as a cat, and I still didn't have a sap to put him down with.

But it was going to be all right.

I sort of walked around the room, and I stopped and looked down in the aquarium at the fish.

The bottom of the tank was covered with marbles.

Marbles are hard, and they are heavy.

I got it at one blink. I went to the medicine cabinet and got the single roll of adhesive tape, then to the closet and got my socks. I put the tape in pieces about four inches long along the window sill. I picked up one of the marbles, laid it on the tape, and then I put another piece of tape on top of it. I kept picking up marbles and adding them until I had a four-inch strip with marbles laid end to end. Then I pinched the tape together around the marbles. When I had nine strips filled with marbles, then I took the rest of the tape and wound it around and around the strips until I had a four-inch thickness of marble. I slipped this into my sock and swung in at the pillow. It made a very satisfying *thunk* and left a neat impression. Would that it would leave the same impression in the head of Sammy!

I got a drink of water from the bathroom, and crawled into bed. Sammy hadn't put any cover over me so I had to slip the blackjack under my right leg. When Sammy came I'd have to get it in my hand and when he bent over I'd have to give him a shot right in the head.

I thought about it for an hour, at least, and then I discovered my hands were shaking and I was scared. It was the pressure. Big time golfers get it.

They play a great game, then there's the ball two feet away from the cup. They can win all the gold monkeys; all they have to do is tap a little white ball. I've seen good golfers miss the whole ball in a situation like that. Same with other sports. Lots of fighters can beat anybody in the world—in a training ring. But when the bright lights hit them, and the crowd is yelling and it's for the money, Liberace could take them.

So, I just had to settle down and think of something else. One thing I could do was think of Ann and Scott. I remembered a trip we'd made on Amtrak to the Rockies. I thought of the time we'd all gone to a camp in Missouri and gotten food poisoning. For a long time I went over the good times and the bad ones too. I'm just a dumb flatfoot, but I knew that the bitterness and the pain that had always risen when they came to my mind had been a cancer, and I knew that in some way I couldn't figure out, Gina and Elvis had been in on the healing of my memories. I thought on that for a long time, then I heard the door open.

I kept my eyes almost closed, but I had to see better this time. Sammy set the tray on the table and I heard him pick the glass off the tray. He had just touched my back with his free hand and started to say, "OK, old buddy. . . ." I opened my eyes and swung on him. He saw my eyes and I have to say he reacted quickly. He pulled his head back so quick I almost missed him, but I got a piece of his forehead and that pound of marbles did its thing. It set him back on his heels and his eyes went blank, one of them looking off to the side. I knew that wouldn't last long, so I rolled off the bed and

his eyes were already beginning to light up. He
started to raise his hands, and I drew back as far as
I could like I was going to throw a rock over the
top of the Washington Monument and smashed
him right between the eyes. He went down like
he'd been hit with a baseball bat. I thought at first
I'd killed him, but he was just out. Blunt instruments are fine for such. Use something sharp and
you just cut people up and make them mad.

I got dressed and then looked down at Sammy,
who wasn't whistling at the moment, and knew I
had to tie him up. I pulled a wire coat hanger off
the rod and unrolled the hook, then straightened
it out. Rolling Sammy over, I took two loops
around his wrists, then wound the ends together
in tight rolls. Forget that noise about the hero
working himself loose. No man can snap a coat-
hanger! He'd cut both hands off at the wrists.

I stuffed a washcloth in his mouth and hoped he
wouldn't throw up, then I went through his pockets. He had what I needed most—a set of car
keys. I walked to the door and noticed that my
home-made blackjack was on the floor beside
Sammy. I picked it up, stared at it for a long time.
Then I looked up and said, "Thanks."

And I meant it.

It had occurred to me that getting out of the
place could be as tough as getting out of the room,
but it was dark, and I saw by the old clock on the
wall that it was three o'clock in the morning. It
was quiet in the hall, and the station in the middle
of it was empty. I figured Sammy was the whole
show, at least on the graveyard shift. I went out the
front door and looked at the sign on the big steel

pole. QUIET HAVEN. I had no idea where I was, but the country is full of small clinics used for drying out those who haven't made the cut. They are usually licensed as rest homes or not licensed at all, and the "nurses" are simply trained to keep law and order while the patient dries out. Lots of them have distinguished people in the little hidden rooms—even some doctors and surgeons who've gotten hooked on drugs from their little black bag. Not a few who are mummified in places like this are those borderline cases of retarded adults. Relatives, if they have money, would rather pay for Uncle Jimmy to be kept sedated at Quiet Haven than have them drooling all over guests. I would guess that such places have a pretty fair working relationship with the local funeral homes because some of the patients never see outside the "clinic" and make only one more trip—to the little room in the back of the funeral parlor, then to the cemetery. Nothing illegal, I guess, and I knew I would probably never look into Quiet Haven in search of a bust.

There were several cars in the small parking lot, but only one was a Ford, a fairly new Mustang. Since Sammy's key was for a Ford, that had to be it. The key worked, and I drove out of the lot onto the street without any idea whether I was in Garland County or Canada. I was driving down a narrow highway, but it was well kept and I knew it must be county or state, so sooner or later I would get somewhere. In five minutes I saw a sign that said *Hot Springs—Five Miles,* and I got my bearings.

I felt pretty bad. My head was swimming and I

kept weaving the Mustang from side to side. Passing over one of the narrow concrete bridges that get you over the lake to the city, I nearly made somebody in a Volkswagen go through the railing.

Dopeheads build up an immunity to drugs and can function pretty well, I guess. But I was feeling like somebody had packed me in molasses. Nothing worked right physically or mentally.

Laboriously I tried to decide what to do. *Can't go home. Sooner or later old Sammy will be found, and then Proctor will come after me again. Can't go to the Vine or to Gina's. Anyone looking for me will find out about that, too.* I got to the edge of town and turned to go to Sonny's place, but then I decided that his place wouldn't be too safe either.

After driving around and getting no better, I finally turned to go to Jack's place. It was the middle of the night, but it was all I could come up with.

All the lights were out, of course, and I was falling down quite a bit as I tried to get up the steps. Finally I crawled up the last of them and decided I'd better ring the doorbell. I'd rung doorbells in my time, heaps of them. But I'd never done it with my head full of exotic lights that flashed off and on, and not with a crazy doorbell that kept moving around every time I made a pass at it. I was being sucked down into that long black tunnel again, and I knew the half-life of the drug they used on me could be very long.

Come on, Delaney, would John Wayne lie here and whimper? Would the Duke quit? No, *siree!* He would sink his fingernails into the cypress walls and pull his entire body upright, then he would

punch the doorbell with his chin. And I respond-
ed to the challenge, folks; I'm a living testimony
that clean living and no candy bars can save
America. I pulled myself up, then I made one pass
at the bell with my hand as I fell backward on the
porch.

It was enough. The next thing I knew the lights
were on and Ameche was saying, "What the hell
are you doing here, Delaney? I nearly shot you."
He pulled me into a sitting position and said, "Are
you drunk?"

"What is it, Jack?" Marie had come out. I
opened my eyes. They were sort of wavering and
shimmering in my sight, so I shut my peepers
hard, and they came into focus.

"Now, Jack, don't get into a snit," I said.

"You are drunk!" he snorted. He pulled me to
my feet and looked into my face. "I never thought
you would take another drink, Ben. Not after the
fight you had with the bottle last time."

"I'm not . . . drunk, Jack. Been shot full of
dope. And it was . . . it was—" I felt as if I were
falling, and I heard Marie saying just before I
went out, "Get him inside, Jack, I think he's sick."

They pulled me in, and they were trying to get
me to bed. I wanted to tell Jack what had happened, so I kept awake, and he and Marie heard
the whole bit.

Finally I wound down, and Jack said, "I don't
get all this, but I'll tell you one thing, Ben, I'll
roust Larry Proctor. He won't have a tail to sit on
after I get through with him."

"No, don't do that, Jack! He knows something

and I want to pry it out of him." I thought of something then: "Will you call the station and see if any word's come in on Taliferro?"

Jack asked with a frown, "You mean Mario Taliferro? What you want with him?"

"Matthews has identified a picture of him. Says he's the one who set him up to take the fall for the killing. If I can get him, he'll talk."

Jack got up and walked around a little, his face was thoughtful. Then he came back and said, "Ben, I've tried to keep you from getting too deep into this. You're a good cop, but I think you've got one thing in your way."

"What thing?"

"You've got that wop girl and that boy on your mind. And you see yourself as some kind of fancy knight with shining armor. You're going to slay the bad old dragon and lay it at their feet. And it won't happen, Ben. Believe me."

"Why not?"

Jack gave me a pitying smile and said, "Because Mario Taliferro is doing a five-year stretch in the pen in California. He's been in for two years, at least a year before the killing. Matthews couldn't have seen him."

I tried to take it in, but it was like ashes in my mouth. "But if that's so, what's Proctor pushing me around for?"

"Ben, you're smarter than that. Everybody knows he's wanted to wipe you out for a long time. And besides that, he works for Lamotta. Didn't you know that?"

I slumped down and muttered, "No." I was getting sick and my head was swimming like a top. "I can't think, Jack. Take me home, or call Sonny and he'll take me."

Marie said firmly, "There'll be none of that. You can make your own decisions when you feel better tomorrow. Tonight you can get a good night's sleep here. Jack, put him in the big guest room. I'll go turn the cover back."

"I can walk!" I snapped as Jack tried to help me down the hall. Then to prove it I fell down flat on my face.

"Yeah, you're in great shape, Delaney," Ameche said, grinning. He pulled me up and walked me into the room where Marie had turned the covers down. "You don't need to go in tomorrow, so says the Chief of Police."

"What day is it?"

"It's the 18th," Marie said. "Now get to bed."

I fell into it, and the old bod just quit on me. The 18th, I thought. Two more days, and George gets it.

I dreamed about the heavy oak chair at Cummins with the electrodes dangling like obscene tentacles.

It was a long night.

13

I slept all night, but sometime before dawn I woke up. No one seemed to be moving around, so I got up and left the house. I was still dressed and the key was still in the Mustang so I took off for town. It was getting light when I got to the shack. I didn't have my gun and some of Proctor's goons might be inside waiting for me, but I didn't really care. Some people spend all their lives and strength getting ready for the ugly circumstance that lies behind the bend ready to sink fangs into them. They plug up all the holes they can, but there's always one tiny door they forget, and the Dark Shadow creeps in and finishes them off. I read about one rich stockbroker in D.C. who spent a fortune in hurricane fences, alarm systems, and bodyguards. One day a single engine Cessna lost power and creamed him as he was getting a tan in his kidney-shaped swimming pool.

I banged my way inside, but there was no waiting. I showered, changed clothes and went to my little arsenal in a niche behind the refrigerator. Most policemen wind up with all the guns they can use. A great many weapons that are taken from the guys in the black hats wind up under some cop's shorts in a drawer. I only had two, one .38 Smith & Wesson and one .44 Magnum Ruger carbine, with a five-round capacity—four in a front tube and one in the chamber. It could fire five 240-grain slugs right through a seven-inch tree. For a weapon a yard long and weighing less than six pounds, it had a reasonable accuracy. I put the .38 in my holster and carried the Ruger out to the Galaxie, got in and started for town.

When I got to the Vine I saw Gina's car parked outside. She must have seen me drive up because she opened the door and met me halfway up the steps. Her face was pale and her hair was messed up like she hadn't had time to fix it. She grabbed me and I was surprised at her grip as she put both arms around me. I held her for just a second, and then she said in a breathy voice like she had been running, "Ben—Ben, we've been just about crazy! Where have you *been?*"

It always feels good to have somebody care about where you've been, and it had been a long time since any woman had. I pulled her back and said, "I got in a mess I couldn't get out of. Are you OK? Is Elvis all right?"

"Yes—you gave me such a scare; Ben, I felt so helpless! Please don't do that again." She held on to my arm as we went inside and Terry was waiting for me.

"You all right, Ben?" I saw most of the kids who

were staying in the house edging in and trying not to move in too fast, but then they couldn't help it and they all made a break and I was surrounded by a bunch of hollering kids!

It wasn't so bad, you know? I'd been pretty hard on some of them—we'd even come to a parting of the ways over house rules—but they were glad to see me.

"Ben, you got to promise us not to get yourself lost like that again," Terry said.

"You want a guarantee, buy a washing machine."

We had breakfast, and as soon as I could I got Gina off to one side and said, "I have to see George. The guy he pointed out has been in the pen for two years."

"Ben—no! But what good will it do?"

"I don't know, but we got until tomorrow to do something." I asked her, "How's Elvis taking it?"

Gina said, "He still says his daddy's coming home. Ben, what will happen if he doesn't?"

"I don't know. Come on, I'll go by the house and you can go with me." I just took it for granted that she would go, and that seemed to please her.

We were on the way out when Earl caught us and said, "Terry says to tell you there's a call for you in the office."

"OK. I'll be right back." I went to the office and picked up the phone. As soon as I said, "Hello," I heard someone either crying or moaning. "I can't hear you, can't you speak up?"

"Ben—Ben—come and get me,—please!" The words faded out but I knew the voice.

"Faye, where are you?"

She didn't answer and I thought she was gone, but then I heard her crying like she was hurt bad. "Ben—don't let them—Ben, come and get me—please."

"I'm coming, Faye, where are you—can you tell me where you are?"

"I don't know—"

"Is there a window there, Faye?"

"Yes—yes—"

"Go look out the window and tell me what you see." While she was gone, my mind raced, trying to figure out a way to locate her. It came to me just as she picked up the phone and said, "Ben, I'm in some kind of a house in the country—and there are trees all around—Ben, I'm so *scared!*"

"Don't worry, Faye, I'll get you, I promise. Now, what's the number on the phone you're using?"

There was a pause and then she said, "235-5521."

"You just sit tight and I'll be there, OK?"

"You promise, Ben?"

"I promise. Is somebody there—who could be dangerous, I mean."

"I think so. Be careful—I know some of them have guns. And—Larry—he's here, and he said he was going to kill you, Ben."

"I'll be careful. Now you just hang up and wait."

I hung up and ran outside. Earl was talking to Gina and I decided to take a chance. "Earl, you want to give me a hand—may be trouble."

He grinned at me and said, "I volunteer. What's the rumble?"

"I'll tell you on the way. Gina, you wait here."

190

"I'm going with you." She had a stubborn little lift to her chin and her eyes challenged me to say no.

We stared at each other for five seconds, daring each other to blink.

"How'd you get so mean?"

"I practice," she said.

We piled in the car and I made a run at Ma Bell. It's pretty tough to get anything out of them, but I went straight to the manager who was having a good time figuring out how to raise the rates again. I shook him up a little when I barged into his office and said, "Gimme an address for this number. I want it now."

He jumped and said, "But what—who are *you?*"

"I haven't got any time to waste. Here's my shield. There's a girl in trouble at this phone. Get me the address in two minutes."

"What's the—ah—girl to you?"

"I'm her—ah—sister." I walked over and helped him up from his desk. He was a big guy, but I hoisted him up like he was stuffed with thistledown. I shoved my face up close to him and said, "You do want to help, don't you?" I squeezed his arm a little and he yelped. Then I helped him sit down again and shoved the phone at him.

He never took his eyes off me while he picked up the phone, dialed a number, and gave it to someone on the other end. Then he listened and said, "The address is 1232 Clearview Drive. That's out in the new addition to the east. Party named Albert Berry."

"Thanks. You can make that call reporting police brutality now."

I got back to the car and pulled out with tires squealing just like Steve McGarret on Hawaii Five-O. I knew the place, and while I got us there I told Earl and Gina the plan. "Earl, you and I are going in after Faye. Gina, you stay outside and get ready to drive us off. We may have to leave in a hurry."

Earl looked happy, and I took the .38 out of the leather and said, "Have you ever shot anybody?"

"Not accidentally," he said, and shoved the gun into his belt. "I got the feeling you want a throw-down just in case."

"What's a *throw-down?*" Gina asked him.

"It's a spare gun that some cops carry. If they shoot someone they throw the gun down and say he was shooting at them."

She stared at me. "Do cops really do that?"

"Some of them." I glanced at her and took in the unbelief on her face. Earl, on the other hand, had a little grin on his wide mouth. "There are bad cops who use throw-downs, just like there are doctors who take out parts that don't need taking out for a fee . . . and preachers who fleece the flock, then run off with the choir director. We build our own myths, I guess, and it comes as a shock to find out that not all mothers have hearts of gold, some sweet old grandmas drink, and some cops are slobs."

I rammed the car into a skid and we headed down a smaller road that led to Berry's place. Neither of them said anything, so I added, "I just have to believe that every time some cop is taking a bribe, there's one turning one down."

Earl asked suddenly, "You really believe that the good guys are gonna win, Delaney?"

I shrugged and said, "I got no proof, but I got the idea that things get settled—but God doesn't always pay off on Saturday night."

"Yeah, well, maybe you're right," Earl said as if it were a new thought. "Where's this place we're going to?"

"House belongs to a hood named Berry. He's never been caught with a smoking gun in his hand, but that's probably just his dumb luck. I think he may have friends there, but I don't want you to shoot unless you have to."

"What if I have to?"

"A man does what he has to do, as John Wayne said about a thousand times."

We were about there and I watched for the signs. It was such an exclusive area that every house was off the road, and the signs marked the names of the owners in old English letters. We came to 1232 and the name Berry, and I said, "We'll leave you here, Gina. Now, if we don't get back in ten minutes, get out of here and call the cops. Promise?"

"Sure, but—be careful, Ben." She suddenly kissed me on the cheek, just as if it was the usual thing, and it sort of made me feel big.

"Come on, Earl." We got out of the car, and I decided to come up from the rear. We scrambled through the brush, getting behind the place with no trouble. There was no sign of movement, and I decided that it was too early for anyone to be up. That's probably how Faye got to use the phone.

"We'll go through the side door," I whispered to Earl. "You stay behind me and keep me covered." I get some of my best stuff from grade-B westerns.

193

We crossed the open area quickly. The door was unlocked and Earl followed me inside. It was a massive room, with a native stone fireplace big enough to roast a Brahma bull, a bar big enough to fill the Long Branch, and beams in the ceiling strong enough to hold up Dallas. It was piled high with post-party debris—glasses on every table, plates with half-eaten sandwiches and tired look-ing olives, coats on the floor. Earl came up beside me and pointed to a Lazy Boy filled to overflow-ing with a fat dude asleep with his mouth wide open. Earl touched me again and motioned down the hall that led off from the living room. "I hear something down there," he whispered.

I nodded and walked over to Sleeping Beauty. I grabbed his Afro with my left hand and gave his head a shake, shoving the Magnum against his teeth at the same time. He opened his eyes and rolled them wildly around until they swung back and focused on the gun, then on me.

"Get up." I stepped back and let him crawl out of the chair, but I kept the muzzle right in his face. "Where's the girl?"

A crafty look came into his pig-eyes. "Girl? I don't know—"

I drew the carbine back and popped it against his mouth, shutting off his words. He put his hands to his mouth, and said, "Now wait a min-ute—"

"A lot of people are into dying these days. You ready to try it?"

I guess he wasn't interested in that, because he immediately said, "Look, I ain't done nothing. The girl's upstairs."

"What's going on down the hall?"

"Still playing poker, I guess. I think you broke a tooth." He looked at me accusingly.

"I'm just a misunderstood war vet. Blame it all on Ho Chi Minh and the local draft board." I shoved him toward the hall and Earl followed us. At the end of the hall was a leather-covered door with GAMEROOM in gold letters. We could hear gambling noises inside. "Here we go," I said to Earl, and opened the door; shoving Fatso in.

We broke in after him and the six guys at the table started to get up when the fat one crashed into the table knocking bottles and glasses off with a crash.

I had seen a couple of them but couldn't remember their names, but I saw that Proctor wasn't there. Al Berry was half out of his chair and he reached suddenly for something in his pocket. I swung the Ruger toward him and it must have been like looking down The Holland Tunnel, because he stopped and broke out into a sweat.

I smiled at him, "Second thoughts are usually best, Al. Where's Proctor?"

"Proctor? I don't know no Proctor!"

"Get up, all of you. Hands against the wall, to coin a phrase." They lined up and I shook them down while Earl kept his .38 ready. Al had a hide-out, a little .32 in his pocket, but the rest were clean. "Al, I don't want any conversation. You got ten fingers. Sometime between the time I break the first one and the time I break the last one you're going to tell me where Proctor and the girl are."

"Now, wait a minute, Delaney—wait a minute!"

Berry said hurriedly. "Look, I don't want no trouble. Proctor brought the girl here—like he's done before. He passed her around to the boys, but she ain't hurt." He spread his hands, "If you got a beef with Larry, take it outta here. He's with the chick upstairs, second door to the right."

"Earl, watch this bunch. I'll get Faye."

"Can we take our hands down?" one of the men asked.

"Keep 'em right there," Earl said. He glanced at me and said, "I'll take care of this end."

The carpet was so thick I didn't think Proctor would hear me, even if he were awake. I stood outside the door turning the knob very slowly and pushed the door open as quiet as I could. The curtains were drawn and it was dark—too dark to see much beyond the shadow of the king-sized bed over by the outside wall. I thought I could see the outline of something under the covers, but when I got there I heard a muffled noise to my right and turned just in time to catch a quick glimpse of Proctor in the corner. He had a gun in his right hand, and I could make out that Faye was trapped in his left arm, his big hand over her mouth to keep her from screaming. He leveled the gun and fired; if I hadn't fallen to the floor he would have got me. I threw up the carbine, but I couldn't take a shot for fear of hitting Faye. He fired again and I kept rolling until I was behind the bed. The third shot ploughed right into the floor in front of my face, so I humped up and made a dive.

It was a dumb play, but there was no other move. He would have got a piece of me with a slug if I stayed there, and I couldn't fire, so I just ran at him. Faye saw me coming and she broke loose at least with one arm. I saw her grab at Proctor's gun arm and pull it down just as I leaped, and his shot went into the floor, I swung the carbine over and down catching him on the forearm. He dropped the gun and Faye squirmed loose. When Proctor stooped to grab the gun with his left hand, I chopped him across the back of the neck with the barrel of the rifle, and he dropped face down without a sound.

"Are you all right, Faye?" I asked. My breath was coming in little pants like it always does after the action is over.

"Yes—but can we get out of here?" I could see a little better now, enough to make out the smudges under her eyes and the large bruise on her left cheekbone. Her eyes were wide, but she didn't seem to be on anything.

"Sure—but I'm taking this with us." I reached down and grabbed Proctor's wrist and began dragging him out of the room. He was a dead-weight but I got him to the stairs, then down with his legs waggling everywhere as he bounded down. I stopped outside the room where Earl was holding the others and said, "Earl, I'll watch them. Go bring the car around, then come in and help me load the garbage."

He left on the run, and no one said anything until we heard the sound of the car pull up and stop. Earl came in and got hold of Proctor's arms, saying, "I'll load him up. You come on when you're ready."

When he had been gone long enough to get Proctor loaded, I said, "You can take your hands down now. I'm leaving and I don't want to see any of you at any windows until we leave. If you do—" I lifted the carbine to wave it at them, "I'll open up on you."

No one answered, and I turned and walked out, and down the hall. I got in the car and laid the gun down on the floorboard. Gina was in the front with her arm around Faye who was now weeping uncontrollably. Gina was making comforting sounds and her lips were broad and maternal as she held the girl. In the back seat Earl was sitting with his feet on Proctor's chest, holding the .38 easily in his big fist. I kept an eye on the windows, but no one showed his face as we pulled out and left the mansion. "Is he dead?" I asked.

"Nah! He's just having quiet time," Earl answered. "You gonna arrest him?"

I didn't answer until the car was off the private road and on the highway headed for Hot Springs. "No. I'm going to interview him."

I knew that Jack and Marie would be looking for me, and I didn't want to be found—not until I had gotten out of Proctor all the information he had in him. The first place they'd look would be my place and the next would be the Vine. I knew one place where no one would look for us. There was a basement to the Vine that could only be entered by a door in the alley. It was on the same electric circuit as the Vine, and we kept some furniture and other junk stored in it, but no one would think of looking for me there, so I went downtown hoping that no prowl cars would spot us.

We pulled up in the alley, and Proctor was waking up. "Let's get him inside quick," I said. We pulled him out of the car and shoved him toward the door. I had a key and as soon as I unlocked it and threw the switch, I told Gina, "Take Faye to my place. I'll either phone or come after you as soon as I take care of this."

"All right, Ben. We'll be waiting."

They took off and I told Earl, "Go in and keep a look out for me. Somebody is sure to come asking where I am. You tell them I took the day off to go fishing. Then come and tell me."

"Sure, Ben." Earl looked at me curiously and then at Proctor. He started to ask a question, then changed his mind and went up the alley.

I dragged Proctor down the stairs and into the damp room lit by a single 40-watt bulb. There were several old sofas with the springs breaking out, a few straight chairs in bad shape and all the old lamps, desks, and so on that we had sorted through to fix the place up. I looked at Proctor, who hadn't said a word, and pushed an old oak desk chair at him right under the naked bulb. "Sit down, Proctor."

"Now—just a minute—you can't do this to me!" he said nervously. I guess I looked pretty grim, and the dark cellar must have made him feel like the guy in *The Cask of Amontillado* that got buried alive. "You want to arrest me, that's OK."

I shoved him down into the chair and pulled the cuffs off the back of my belt. I went behind him, and when he tried to get away I tapped him with the barrel of the Ruger that I'd brought with me. "Sit still." I put one arm through the slats, brought the other on the outside, and clamped the cuffs on his wrists. Then I laid the gun down and pulled a battered old chair in front of him and sat down.

"Larry, I want some answers. You are going to the station. You'll be charged with kidnapping and assault and anything else I can think of."

"Kidnapping! She came of her own free will!"

"I'll testify different, and so will Earl. And maybe even Al Berry will have a few words—with the proper kind of persuasion. You've never been in a state prison, have you, Larry? It's pretty bad. Food is bad; terrible social life. Way I heard a guy tell it, prisons don't cure nothing but heterosexuality."

"Delaney, you gotta be reasonable!" Even in the dim light I could see that he was pale and there was a fine sheen of sweat on his handsome face. He leaned forward and his voice was cracking as he said, "OK, so maybe I took the girl there to Barry's—but she asked for it when she came to me in the first place. You'll never make it stick! Not in court!"

"You won't get much, I'll give you that. But you know I'll do my best to see you get something. And even six months in Cummins can do bad things to a guy like you."

I saw he was breaking a little, but I didn't have time to play games with him. "Besides, Larry, it's not just what happens to you after you get to the station you got to worry about." I didn't say anything else, but took out a pocket knife and tested it on my thumb. Proctor's eyes went wide and he watched as I toyed with the blade. I kept my mouth shut and let his imagination begin to slice him up a little inside.

200

"I tell you, Delaney, I don't know anything."

Nothing in the Bible against acting that I know of, and this punk had to believe I had the will to make him talk. I reached into his pocket, pulled out a lighter I could see through the fabric, lit it, and held the tip of the blade in it until it turned cherry red.

"You'll talk, punk. You'll be wishing you had *more* to tell me pretty soon." I just made a small movement toward him and he went all to pieces.

"Wait—what is it? What d' you want?" he began to shake and tears ran down his face.

"You were in a game with Vito about a year ago."

"Yeah, sure, I was in lots of them."

"In this one a guy came in and got cleaned of about $500 in just a few hands, then he left."

"I don't—yeah, I do remember that. Guy was a real dummy, but I didn't do it. Wasn't even in the game."

"That's what I want to know. Who was in the game?"

"Well, I can't remember too good, there was Leland Thornton, Dutch Frazier, and Vito—and let's see, oh, yeah, there was Jocko Parelli."

"Who else?"

"That's all—wait a minute—there was one other guy, but I didn't know him. I guess he was just floating through."

There it was. The one thing I had to have just couldn't be gotten out of Proctor because it wasn't there. I had one more idea.

"Larry, if you can tell me one thing, I maybe will forget to take you in." He nodded so hard his teeth clicked. "I know you got something to do with Bernie Floyd. Where is he?" I popped the lighter on and put the blade in the flame again, and it hypnotized Proctor. He'd started to shake his head, but the sight of the cherry blade stopped him.

"Yeah, well—I keep in touch. He's in Little Rock now. I got his number."

I didn't let him see what good news that was, but I unlocked his cuffs and said, "Come on."

"Where we going?"

"You're going to make a phone call."

I shut him up and led him to a phone booth on the corner. I said, "Let's have the number." He fished it out of his billfold and read it off. I plugged the phone with a dime and dialed the number. "You tell Bernie it's OK to come back. Then you can go."

Bernie must have been sitting on the phone, because Larry said quickly, "Hey, is this you, Bernie? Yeah—Larry. What? No, there's nothing wrong. I just called to say it's OK for you to come back now."

I pulled the phone away from his ear enough to hear Floyd say, "What about Delaney?" And I covered the phone and whispered, "Tell him I been run off the department. Left town."

"Delaney got fired," Proctor said. "He's gone."

"Tell him to go back to his house. You want to see him."

He relayed this to Floyd and then at another whisper said, "Come on now, Bernie. Call me from your place."

I took the receiver from him and plunked it

down. "OK, punk, you can go back to your sewer now."

Proctor looked different. He was a no-good bum who had hurt his share, but I didn't think he'd be quite as tough any more. Once you get bled dry as he'd been, it takes a long time to get over it—and I didn't think Proctor was the type who could come back.

I watched him hurry out of the alley, and I went to the Vine and found Earl resting in a chair eating donuts and drinking coffee.

"Earl, I hate to ask you, but I got nobody else. I got to have a place watched."

He shoved a bunch of donuts in a paper sack and filled a large plastic cup with coffee. "I'm ready." He cocked his head at me and grinned, then he said, "Nobody ever told me it was so exciting being a Christian, Delaney."

I was still pretty woozy from all the drugs I'd taken in, but I managed to grin back and say, "Well, you mustn't count on having such good fun every day."

I borrowed the old van that the Vine owns and took Earl to Bernie's place. "Soon as somebody shows—anybody—don't mess with them. Just call me. Got a dime?" He had, and I showed him the drugstore down the street. I left him hidden behind a large shrub, munching the donuts across the street from Bernie's place.

I had no business driving. My head was swimming, and it hurt too. By the time I got to my place I was just about ready to drop. I went inside and Gina was there, but Faye wasn't.

"Some of the girls from the Vine came and got

her," Gina explained. "I think she'll be all right. She had a pretty rough time, Ben. I think it was the worse she's ever had, and she's not the same. We talked for a long time. . . . Do you think she can change, Ben?"

"Anybody can change, I guess." My head was swimming and I sat down suddenly. "I got only one real thought about that—people do what they want to do. People who want to go to school, they go to school. May have to wait tables and do without a car, but they go if they want to. People who want to fish find a way to fish. People who want to go to church, they go to church."

"I guess that's right," Gina said slowly. She shook her head and sat down beside me. "There's no hope for George. You wanted to do that, get him out, I mean—and you can't do it." She put her hand on my arm and said quickly, "Oh, I'm not blaming you, Ben! I just mean, there are some things that just don't happen."

"Yeah, it shoots holes in my little theory." I lay back on the bed; the room had started swimming in an alarming fashion. "I don't think I can stay awake. Look, we got one chance. The phone may ring and I'll miss it if I'm out. Will you stay here and get me up if it does ring?"

I was already falling out and her voice seemed to come from far away: "You sleep, Ben. I'll be here." I think she said something else and called me something that Ann used to call me a long time ago, but I was falling, falling into the same old tunnel.

14

When I finally woke up it was dark; I saw by the clock that it was nearly eight. A reading lamp on my tiny desk was on and I saw that Gina was reading a book. My mouth tasted like the inside of a bird cage, and a bunch of demented elves were doing a number on my head with pickaxes, but I wasn't thickheaded from the drugs.

Gina was engrossed in the book and I enjoyed watching her. The hard lines were erased, and she just looked very young and vulnerable. "Why didn't you wake me up?" I asked, getting off the bed.

"Oh, Ben," she smiled and putting the book down she came over to stand beside me. "I thought you needed sleep—and Earl hasn't called yet. Let me fix you something to eat."

"Sounds good—and I'll cut these whiskers off." I went into the bathroom and shaved. I gave my most charming smile at the mirror but the image in the mirror had eyes that looked like two burnt holes in a blanket. *You're a sight, Delaney. If they put your picture in a cornfield, the crows would bring back corn they stole two years ago.*

I went to the table and we pitched into the eggs and ham that Gina had scared up. "You do eggs good," I said. "And the coffee's just right."

"Yeah, I like to cook. Used to, that is." She started to say something else, but the phone rang and I lunged out of my chair to yank it off the hook.

"Hello, is that you, Ben?" Earl said before I could speak.

"Yeah, what's going on?"

"There's a little bird in the nest. Came in about ten minutes ago."

"OK, I'll be there in about ten minutes. He come in a car?"

"Nah, a black-and-white." It caught me off-guard. A police car? I felt like I'd stepped into a pothole. Then suddenly a crazy idea nudged at me. But I pushed it away.

"Go back and get behind your shrub. I'll come walking in from the south. You stay put—but if I don't come out in fifteen minutes, call the law. Got it?"

"Right."

I hung up and put my holster on, and by the time I was to the door, Gina was with me. "You're not leaving me, Ben."

"You're harder to throw away than a boomerang!" I complained. "OK, you can come, but do exactly what I say."

"Sure. I just want to go with you."

We made the drive staying inside the speed limits, and I came in from the south. We parked the car and walked toward Floyd's place. There was no car outside that I could see, but as we got even with the house I glanced across the street and caught a glimpse of Earl leaning out from behind the hedge; I gave him a wave and we went up on the porch. "Stay a little behind me," I whispered to Gina.

I started to use a jimmy, but the door was unlocked and I pushed it open and stepped inside. Gina followed me and we could see by the light that was on in a room down the hall.

It was sort of a dog-trot arrangement, with a short hall running the length of the house. There were two doors on each side, and a light shone from the second door on the left. There was no sound that I could hear, but I knew Floyd had to be up, so I pulled my gun and waved Gina to stand beside the front door. The house was old, and as I made my way down the hall there was no way to stop the old timbers from creaking. Floyd wasn't known to be a gunman, but who knew for sure? He could have been waiting in that room with a sawed-off shotgun ready to shoot at anything that came at him.

There are thousands of boring hours in police work, but every once in a while the work gets interesting—going into a dark alley looking for some hophead or walking into a room like this one. It goes with the territory, and I'd had two good friends who went in alive and came out dead.

I could sneak in, or make a jump at it, and I

decided on the last. I just tippy-toed to the door, waited to see if I could hear anyone breathing, swung through the doorframe, held my gun in both hands, and froze.

Bernie Floyd wasn't going anywhere.

Not ever.

He lay on the floor with that odd eloquent gesture that the violently murdered often achieve—on his back with one arm flung outward and the other clutching at the crimson stain that blossomed across his chest. I stepped over and knelt beside him, noting the Colt .45 that lay almost hidden under his outflung arm. He was still warm, couldn't have been dead more than a few minutes, and that went over me quick—like touching a live wire. I started to get up, but there was someone behind me. I had my back to the door, and he must have been waiting in the room across the hall. Time seemed to flatten out and my only thought was of Gina. If he got me, he'd have to get her too. Just as I was primed to throw myself to one side and hope to get off at least a crippling shot before he got me, he spoke.

"Hold it! Freeze—and drop that gun!"

I let the gun fall and got to my feet. I turned around slowly and faced him.

Ameche was framed in the doorway with the Colt Python zeroed in on my chest. His face was hard, eyes glittering and a faint sheen of sweat on his forehead. He ran his tongue around his lips as he saw me, then blurted out, "Ben! What are you doing here?" He lowered the gun and took a step toward me, then brought it up again as Gina came running into the room. She saw Floyd's body and caught at my arm, her face the color of wallpaper paste.

"Hello, Jack," I said, then looked down at the corpse. "You got Bernie I see."

"Yeah," he nodded slowly, and he looked at me intently. "You were right all the time, Ben. He's the one who killed the Taylor girl."

"How'd you find out?" I asked.

Ameche grinned and put his gun away. "I been cutting you down, but I've been doing a little snooping on my own. I got suspicious when he claimed the reward, so I did a little investigation myself. Then when I found out he left town, I had an undercover man in the Little Rock area get acquainted. He kept me posted, then tonight he called and said Floyd had gotten drunk and bragged about killing the girl, then about pulling down the reward."

"He tell you that Bernie was coming back to-night?"

"More or less. Said he was leaving—so I took a chance and drove by his place."

"How'd he get the drop on you?"

"I got careless," Ameche shrugged. "When I told him he was under arrest, he said he had a bundle, for me, you know? Then he showed me the panel up there." Over the sink was an old-fashioned cabinet, and built in between the cabinet and the ceiling was a small hole. A panel had been removed and stood open. "He pulled the panel off and reached in to get the money, but he came out with the .45."

"What—what does it mean, Ben?" Gina asked.

"It means that Matthews won't die," Jack said.

"I better get a call to the governor right away."

He half turned to go when he had finished, and Gina gave a little cry of joy. But when I stooped to pick up my gun, I glanced at Jack and he had wheeled to face me. I had reached my hand out for the Special but as our eyes locked, Jack must have sensed something, because he raised his gun and said, "Don't touch it, Ben." He looked at me for a long moment, then said sadly, "I didn't think you'd buy it, Ben. You're too smart."

I stood up and shrugged. "You left too many tracks."

He watched me carefully, and the gun was steady in his big fist. He gave his massive head a small shake, and the lines at the edge of his mouth grew deeper. "I wish you had kept out of it, Ben. I really wish you'd kept out of it."

"What—what's wrong?" Gina asked nervously. She saw the gun pointed at me and her face grew pale. "Aren't you going to call the governor?"

Ameche paid no attention to her, but asked as if it didn't matter much, "How'd you get it?"

I reached slowly into my shirt pocket and pulled out the photograph of Taliferro. "This was the tip-off." I held it out hoping it would catch his attention, but he never blinked. "We were all looking at Taliferro, and George is too dumb to tell us which *guy* it was that set him up."

Gina leaned forward and looked at the picture. "Why—it's *you!*" She stared at Ameche. "You're the policeman making the arrest!"

Jack said, "You didn't nail me from that, did you, Ben?"

"No. I searched this whole place a couple of

days ago. I found that little spot—" I nodded to the hole in the cabinet hoping Jack would glance at it—"and there wasn't anything there. No money and no gun."

Jack's eyes never moved. "Anything else?"

"Well, I figured that nobody but someone who was a friend would have gone to so much trouble to get rid of me without knocking me off. Vito and Proctor wanted to do it, but they didn't." I was trying to gauge the distance I had to move to get a chop at the gun, and I needed about six inches. I took one of those inches by shifting my feet and he didn't notice. "My guess is they wanted to finish me off—and you wouldn't let them."

"That's right, Ben. I thought I could keep you from digging. But I didn't make it."

I took another inch and threw my arms out to conceal it: "Why'd you do it, Jack? Set Matthews up?"

"I got into Vito for a bundle," he shrugged, and I nudged another half inch in his direction.

"It all seemed to come together, Ben. I'd just gotten the goods on Bernie, and the next night I ran across Matthews in the poker game. I saw how easy it would be to use Bernie and collect the reward. Bernie knew I could bail him any time, so he'd keep his nose clean. Matthews was dying anyway. Who'd it hurt, Ben?"

"Can't see it that way, Jack. Even if you did feel like that, what about his cut?"

"I guess we're wasting time," Jack murmured. "I'm sorry it's come to this, Ben. You know it would kill Marie to find out I'm a crook."

He was winding up to let us have it and I had to

take a chance or even a piece of one. "There's a guy watching the place, Jack. He saw you come in. You shoot and he'll be a witness. How would Marie feel if you were a murderer?"

It worked a little. He cut his eyes toward the front of the house, which he couldn't see, but it was all I was going to get. I was leaned forward on the balls of my feet and I fell at him reaching out as far as I could to get a piece of the gun.

I almost made it. One inch too short, and Ameche had reactions like a steel trap. He brought the gun up, and I was never closer to the Big Jump. I saw his trigger finger whiten; his eyes were like open graves. Then Gina's scream caught at him, and she had what Churchill would have called her finest hour.

She had been standing close, but when she saw the gun aimed at me, she stepped in front of me, turning her back to Jack, and waiting for the bullet.

There's a picture for my little gallery of good things. She was shaking as if she had a fever and her face was pale as ashes. But she had put me first. Pretty fine.

Jack was staring at her as if he couldn't believe his eyes. He's seen a lot of hard things in his life, and I don't think he'd have backed up from anything that moved. But the sight of Gina trying to take a bullet for ugly ole Delaney seemed to paralyze him.

The silence ran on, and I said, "Jack, she can't hurt you. Who'd believe anything she said?" I didn't argue, but there was a break in the bleakness in Jack's face, and the gun went down a fraction of an inch.

He looked across her head at me and said, "Ben, is there really a guy out there?"

I looked him right in the eye and said, "Yes. He's been watching to tell me when Floyd got back."

There was a little shifting of the scales then, as Ameche put things together. Then he sighed and his eyes seemed to come to life. "You can't hurt me either, Ben." He stared at me and added, "You're the only guy in the world whose word I'd take for this. But I give you a choice. You tell me you're out of it—you and the girl go free. We make a call and Matthews is out. The ten grand you get can go to him if you want."

"And if I don't?"

"You will," Ameche gave a grim smile. "You may be religious, but you're not stupid."

"You got my word, Jack." I looked at him and said good-bye to the best friend I'd ever had.

As we looked at each other over Floyd's corpse there was another death—death of a relationship. No matter if we worked together, hunted together, whatever. I'd lost a few friends to the grave, but nothing was harder than this, for I had trusted Jack, had loved him, though neither of us had ever said it like that. When love dies it's messy and gut-wrenching, and neither of us wanted to hold a post-mortem.

"I'll call the troops," Jack said. He wheeled and left without a backward look.

I got Gina out of there. Earl joined us from his

look-out spot and we drove away. On the way back to town we passed a police car headed for Floyd's at full speed. "Did anyone go in besides the one guy, Earl?"

"No," he said quickly, "Unless it was while I was gone to the phone."

"I guess it was then," I murmured. Earl looked mystified, but we put him out at the Vine. "You've been great, Earl. I'll see you later." He gave me a wide grin and we watched him go into the Vine in that swinging walk of his.

I drove very slowly toward Gina's place, and finally she broke the silence. "Jack—he's behind it all?"

I didn't want to think about it, but she had to know. "You won't read it in the *Sentinel*, but he was behind it."

"But won't he be arrested?" She was over her fear and rage was beginning to build up. "He's a killer, isn't he?"

"Floyd is a killer. I'm pretty sure the gun beside him will be the one that killed Helen Taylor. He was resisting arrest when he was killed. No one can prove there's any link between Floyd and Jack. Lamotta and Proctor might think so, but who's going to take their word against a police chief?"

She was quiet for a long time, and I pulled her closer to me. "Look, think of it this way—George will be coming home right away. Think how that'll make Elvis happy, and Elizabeth."

"I guess so—but it's not fair!"

I felt pretty bad, but I laughed as best as I could

and gave her a hug. "You want rules, you should take up checkers. There's these little squares and these little round things. And it's all so easy. No angels or demons on the board—just squares and circles and keep the rules."

She smiled and leaned against me, "Well, I guess you're trying to tell me that things don't end happily ever after."

"Some things do, Gina. A few." We were pulling into the yard and there was Elvis swinging back and forth in an old tire tied by a frayed rope to a spindly limb of an aging sycamore in the postage-stamp front yard.

"Ben," Gina asked, "when it looked like Jack was going to shoot both of us, you know what I thought?"

"What?"

"Two things. First I thought, *I've blown it all!* You know, everything seems pretty minor when you're about to die. So, I . . . I wished I'd paid more attention to what Terry was saying at the Vine. And I wished I'd . . . lived different." She looked up at me as we eased toward the curb. "Do you think it's too late, too late for me?"

I looked down into her face and said, "Not too late. Not for you."

She thought about that, then turned to face me. "What about Elvis—and what about George? I . . . I don't see how it can all come out, Ben. Can you?"

There it was, the old question. I looked over to where Elvis was slowly going around in the swing. "Gina, look at Elvis. See, he's wound that swing up and now he's letting it spin until he gets dizzy. I must have done that a million times when I was a kid."

"Sure. Me too. I guess everyone tries that when they're little."

"Well, I guess even Moses and David did something like that—and now they're gone. Every time I look at old pictures of the Civil War it makes me feel funny, you know, to see the faces of those young boys who went off to fight. I see some fourteen- or fifteen-year-old all dressed up in his new uniform; then I find out that he died at Shiloh or Gettysburg. But it came to me one day: they're all gone, Gina—all those boys and all their sweethearts and wives. All the presidents and kings. Just like Elvis will be gone one day—and George." I gave her a little touch and said, "Just like you and I will be gone."

"That's so sad!" she said quietly, and her eyes were damp.

"Sure it is—if you think this world is all of it."

She looked up at me and whispered, "That's what you've been saying to me, isn't it, Ben? That's what made you different."

"Yeah, it is." I nodded toward Elvis, and said, "I don't know how long Elvis has. I don't know how long I have, but this world's not all of it, Gina. It can't be."

"I—I'm just not good enough to be a Christian," she said.

"You know, I guess that's what everybody says at first—and I guess it's what got me started. I noticed that Jesus Christ never turned anybody away. No matter how bad or rotten they'd been, he made a place for them. I can't explain it, Gina, but if you've got a want to, there'll be a place."

She was very still and very quiet, and then she raised her face to me and said so softly I almost missed it: "I've got a want to, Ben."

"Then you'll find the way."

"But what about us, Ben?" she asked suddenly.

"Well, I guess we might end up like Mr. Dillon and Miss Kitty—just real good buddies and all that."

"Nooo, I don't think so, Ben." She tapped her chin with a slender finger and said thoughtfully, "I never thought I'd do a thing like that—trying to take a bullet for a big ugly cop."

"Ugliness is in the eye of the beholder," I said, then gave her a kiss. Elvis had spotted us and was flying over to the car.

"Your daddy's coming home, Elvis!" Gina said, giving him a hug.

His finely featured face was filled with surprise and he just gave a little frown and said, "Well, *sure* he is, Gina. I told you I asked God for that."

Gina grabbed him and as she hugged him fiercely, she looked at me over his thin shoulder, saying, "Well, I've got some things you can arrange for me when you have time."

Looking at them, I remembered that I'd always held that the biggest lie in the storybook was the one that says, "And they got married and lived happily ever after."

So I was *wrong!* What does a dumb cop know about stuff like that?

Other Living Books Bestsellers

THE BEST CHRISTMAS PAGEANT EVER by Barbara Robinson. A delightfully wild and funny story about what can happen to a Christmas program when the "horrible Herdman" family of brothers and sisters are miscast in the roles of the Christmas story characters from the Bible. 07–0137 $2.50.

ELIJAH by William H. Stephens. He was a rough-hewn farmer who strolled onto the stage of history to deliver warnings to Ahab the king and to defy Jezebel the queen. A powerful biblical novel you will never forget. 07–4023 $3.50.

THE TOTAL MAN by Dan Benson. A practical guide on how to gain confidence and fulfillment. Covering areas such as budgeting of time, money matters, and marital relationships. 07–7289 $3.50.

HOW TO HAVE ALL THE TIME YOU NEED EVERY DAY by Pat King. Drawing from her own and other women's experiences as well as from the Bible and the research of time experts, Pat has written a warm and personal book for every Christian woman. 07–1529 $2.95.

IT'S INCREDIBLE by Ann Kiemel. "It's incredible" is what some people say when a slim young woman says, "Hi, I'm Ann," and starts talking about love and good and beauty. As Ann tells about a Jesus who can make all the difference in their lives, some call that incredible, and turn away. Others become miracles themselves, agreeing with Ann that it's incredible. 07–1818 $2.50.

EVERGREEN CASTLES by Laurie Clifford. A heartwarming story about the growing pains of five children whose hilarious adventures teach them unforgettable lessons about love and forgiveness, life and death. Delightful reading for all ages. 07–0779 $3.50.

JOHN, SON OF THUNDER by Ellen Gunderson Traylor. Travel with John down the desert paths, through the courts of the Holy City, and to the foot of the cross. Journey with him from his luxury as a privileged son of Israel to the bitter hardship of his exile on Patmos. This is a saga of adventure, romance, and discovery — of a man bigger than life — the disciple "whom Jesus loved." 07–1903 $3.95.

WHAT'S IN A NAME? compiled by Linda Francis, John Hartzel, and Al Palmquist. A fascinating name dictionary that features the literal meaning of people's first names, the character quality implied by the name, and an applicable Scripture verse for each name listed. Ideal for expectant parents! 07–7935 $2.95.

Other Living Books Bestsellers

THE MAN WHO COULD DO NO WRONG by Charles E. Blair with John and Elizabeth Sherrill. He built one of the largest churches in America ... then he made a mistake. This is the incredible story of Pastor Charles E. Blair, accused of massive fraud. A book "for error-prone people in search of the Christian's secret for handling mistakes." 07–4002 $3.50.

GIVERS, TAKERS AND OTHER KINDS OF LOVERS by Josh McDowell. This book bypasses vague generalities about love and sex and gets right down to basic questions: Whatever happened to sexual freedom? What's true love like? What is your most important sex organ? Do men respond differently than women? If you're looking for straight answers about God's plan for love and sexuality then this book was written for you. 07–1031 $2.50.

MORE THAN A CARPENTER by Josh McDowell. This best selling author thought Christians must be "out of their minds." He put them down. He argued against their faith. But eventually he saw that his arguments wouldn't stand up. In this book, Josh focuses upon the person who changed his life — Jesus Christ. 07–4552 $2.50.

HIND'S FEET ON HIGH PLACES by Hannah Hurnard. A classic allegory which has sold more than a million copies! 07–1429 $3.50.

THE CATCH ME KILLER by Bob Erler with John Souter. Golden gloves, black belt, green beret, silver badge. Supercop Bob Erler had earned the colors of manhood. Now can he survive prison life? An incredible true story of forgiveness and hope. 07–0214 $3.50.

WHAT WIVES WISH THEIR HUSBANDS KNEW ABOUT WOMEN by Dr. James Dobson. By the best selling author of *DARE TO DISCIPLINE* and *THE STRONG-WILLED CHILD*, here's a vital book that speaks to the unique emotional needs and aspirations of today's woman. An immensely practical, interesting guide. 07–7896 $2.95.

PONTIUS PILATE by Dr. Paul Maier. This fascinating novel is about one of the most famous Romans in history — the man who declared Jesus innocent but who nevertheless sent him to the cross. This powerful biblical novel gives you a unique insight into the life and death of Jesus. 07–4852 $3.95.

BROTHER OF THE BRIDE by Donita Dyer. This exciting sequel to *THE BRIDE'S ESCAPE* tells of the faith of a proud, intelligent Armenian family whose Christian heritage stretched back for centuries. A story of suffering, separation, valor, victory, and reunion. 07–0179 $2.95.

LIFE IS TREMENDOUS by Charlie Jones. Believing that enthusiasm makes the difference, Jones shows how anyone can be happy, involved, relevant, productive, healthy, and secure in the midst of a high-pressure, commercialized, automated society. 07–2184 $2.50.

HOW TO BE HAPPY THOUGH MARRIED by Dr. Tim LaHaye. One of America's most successful marriage counselors gives practical, proven advice for marital happiness. 07–1499 $2.95.

Other Living Books Bestsellers

DAVID AND BATHSHEBA by Roberta Kells Dorr. Was Bathsheba an innocent country girl or a scheming adulteress? What was King David really like? Solomon — the wisest man in the world — was to be king, but could he survive his brothers' intrigues? Here is an epic love story which comes radiantly alive through the art of a fine storyteller. 07–0618 $3.95.

TOO MEAN TO DIE by Nick Pirovolos with William Proctor. In this action-packed story, Nick the Greek tells how he grew from a scrappy immigrant boy to a fearless underworld criminal. Finally caught, he was imprisoned. But something remarkable happened and he was set free — truly set free! 07–7283 $3.50.

FOR WOMEN ONLY. This bestseller gives a balanced, entertaining, diversified treatment of all aspects of womanhood. Edited by Evelyn and J. Allan Petersen, founder of Family Concern. 07–0897 $3.50.

FOR MEN ONLY. Edited by J. Allan Petersen, this book gives solid advice on how men can cope with the tremendous pressures they face every day as fathers, husbands, workers. 07–0892 $3.50.

ROCK. What is rock music really doing to you? Bob Larson presents a well-researched and penetrating look at today's rock music and rock performers. What are lyrics really saying? Who are the top performers and what are their life-styles? 07–5686 $2.95.

THE ALCOHOL TRAP by Fred Foster. A successful film executive was about to lose everything — his family's vacation home, his house in New Jersey, his reputation in the film industry, his wife. This is an emotion-packed story of hope and encouragement, offering valuable insights into the troubled world of high pressure living and alcoholism. 07–0078 $2.95.

LET ME BE A WOMAN. Best selling author Elisabeth Elliot (author of *THROUGH GATES OF SPLENDOR*) presents her profound and unique perspective on womanhood. This is a significant book on a continuing controversial subject. 07–2162 $2.95.

WE'RE IN THE ARMY NOW by Imeldia Morris Eller. Five children become their older brother's "army" as they work together to keep their family intact during a time of crisis for their mother. 07–7862 $2.95.

WILD CHILD by Mari Hanes. A heartrending story of a young boy who was abandoned and struggled alone for survival. You will be moved as you read how one woman's love tames this boy who was more animal than human. 07–8224 $2.95.

THE SURGEON'S FAMILY by David Hernandez with Carole Gift Page. This is an incredible three-generation story of a family that has faced danger and death — and has survived. Walking dead-end streets of violence and poverty, often seemingly without hope, the family of David Hernandez has struggled to find a new kind of life. 07–6684 $2.95.

The books listed are available at your bookstore. If unavailable, send check with order to cover retail price plus 10% for postage and handling to:

Tyndale House Publishers, Inc.
Box 80
Wheaton, Illinois 60189

Prices and availability subject to change without notice. Allow 4–6 weeks for delivery.